This book is to be returned on or before the last date stamped below.

Books should be returned or renewed by the last date stamped above

MP

WHEN TOMORROW COMES

Kate was delighted to be offered a job on Dartmoor, looking after a house whilst the owners were away. It would be a refuge for her and her little boy, Josef — she was terrified that her ex-husband would kidnap his son and take him back to the Middle East. In Devon, Kate is beginning to feel secure — until she gives shelter to an escaped prisoner and nurses him back to health. But Kate isn't looking for love, just a place of safety . . .

PATRICIA FREER

WHEN TOMORROW COMES

Complete and Unabridged

LINFORD
Leicester

First published in Great Britain

First Linford Edition
published 1999

British Library CIP Data

Freer, Patricia
    When tomorrow comes.—Large print ed.—
Linford romance library
1. Love stories
2. Large type books
I. Title
823.9'14 [F]

ISBN 0–7089–5546–0

Published by
F. A. Thorpe (Publishing) Ltd.
Anstey, Leicestershire

Set by Words & Graphics Ltd.
Anstey, Leicestershire
Printed and bound in Great Britain by
T. J. International Ltd., Padstow, Cornwall

This book is printed on acid-free paper

1

The advertisement seemed like a life-line! It offered what Kate desperately needed. A bolt hole for the winter where her pursuers wouldn't think of looking for her — at a price she could afford.

Retirees, chasing the sun, wish to rent out isolated country home in Devon for six months, to someone who will care for pets. No charge to right person except household bills.

She had written off immediately. Could this be the miracle she had hoped for? She hardly dared hope it was. There was bound to be a flaw. Life had taught her not to believe in miracles!

The answer came by telephone to her friend Anna's London flat, where she and Josef had found temporary refuge. The voice on the other end of the line had warmth and a West Country burr.

'Mrs Lennox?'

'Yes.' Kate was breathless with hope. Lennox was not her real name. Her naturally honest nature balked at lying, but she had had to get used to it. In any case, her married surname was difficult for English tongues to wind themselves around, and she was like a tigress where Josef was concerned. Nothing was more important than his safety!

The caller was reassuringly succinct.

'Jim Carney here. We received your letter. My wife and I — we wondered if you'd like to come down for a few days — with a view to taking up the post. Meet each other — and see what it entails.'

'I'd love to.' Kate could hardly get the words out, she was so anxious. 'Are you sure it would be all right — a small boy in the house?' she asked.

The deep voice chuckled. 'We've got grandchildren of our own. Scattered all over the globe, more's the pity. Will you drive down or come by train?'

'I don't have my own car, so it will

have to be the train.'

She didn't want to sound in too much of a hurry, but she had been at Anna's some time. They might be close behind her. Getting away soon could be important.

Tentatively she asked, 'Will tomorrow be too soon?'

He was immediately and comfortingly accepting of her hurry.

'Tomorrow will be just fine. Take the ten thirty from Paddington and I'll meet you at Plymouth.'

He sounded so solid, so reassuringly normal. Once he had rung off, Kate began to wish that the job could be in the presence, rather than the absence of the Carney's. A man like that would be so strong, so fatherly!

For the first time in years she remembered her grief at the death of her parents when she was still at school. Perhaps if they had been alive she might never have been foolish enough to marry Sirius. With no-one to guide her, he had dazzled her with his dark, foreign urgency and good looks. She had paid for her illusions though — and paid heavily! Firstly when they had gone to the Middle East and she had discovered, with growing horror, what it was like to be the wife in such a totally different culture.

Back with his rich and arrogant family, who had not even tried to welcome or accept her, Sirius had changed completely and begun to treat her badly — ashamed of the very Englishness that had made her interesting to him before.

His professed love had quickly faded. Hers had turned to fear, because soon he began striking her regularly, sometimes simply for failing to understand some of the things expected of her. Eventually life became so impossible that she knew she had to get away.

Before a way presented itself, however, she had become pregnant. Even then she thought there might be hope. Perhaps a child would make the family begin to include her in their closed circle. Perhaps fatherhood would make Sirius kinder — maybe even love her again!

Then Josef was born and Kate realised that she had never known — or dreamed of — the encompassing passion of mother love. She was besotted with her baby.

She could not believe it when she was told, scathingly by her husband, and her father-in-law, that her child was a source of shame to them, for it's mixed blood. How could anyone not adore this beautiful child?

Nevertheless, her conscience was clear after that. Father or not, somehow she would take the baby home with her.

She had been lucky! A party of English tourists had helped her cross the border with them, and go back to her own country.

Thankfully, she had made contact with old family and college friends, like Anna, who had helped her in her divorce.

Then came the bombshell! Sirius, far

from being relieved at her going, was incensed. When he was contacted by the lawyer, all hell had been let loose!

Apparently forgetting his previous attitude, he vowed to snatch Josef from her. With the resources of his family money at his disposal, Kate knew that the only thing she could do was keep running.

They had been fugitives ever since, changing names, staying a while, then moving on. She ached for peace and a chance to bring Josef up in a stable environment.

It was a nightmare to which she could see no end. The chase was made out of nothing other than spite and malice, but Sirius and his henchmen seemed always to discover where she was and be close behind her. Threatening letters and phone calls to her friends and relatives were always a signal for her to move on, often at night.

Surely they could have no reason to believe she would go to Devon, though?

★ ★ ★

The journey, next day, was a pleasant one. With her usual vigilance, Kate scanned the travellers on Paddington station and the train, but there were no dark, young men, no watchers, no sense of being spied on. By the time they reached Plymouth, she was relatively relaxed — and Josef was enchanted by the journey past the boats and sea-birds along the coastline.

'Look, Mummy, look, there's another one diving. Its head is right down in the mud.'

And later he gasped, 'Ooh, the earth is all red — and we're going into it — through a tunnel.'

When they stepped down on to the platform, there was no mistaking her host. Big, bluff, tweed-capped and wearing an anorak, Jim Carney was exactly as she had imagined him. He picked up Josef, settled him on one arm and, with the other took her large suitcase from her. They went towards the exit, he talking all the while.

'Hope you like pasties. My wife's been busy in the kitchen all morning. They're as big as dinner-plates. She's thrilled to have a kiddie to cook something for. It's been a long time since ours were here,' he frowned slightly before smiling at Josef in a way that brightened up his whole face. 'This little fellow looks as though he could do with a bit of filling up — you, too, m'dear, come to that. You're as thin as a rake.'

Kate watched wryly as Josef, who had always been warned not to talk to strangers, responded immediately to this big, friendly man. On the journey to the farm he prattled endlessly, informing Mr Carney, in some detail, about the things he had seen from the train.

Once there, however, he was struck dumb with delight!

It was partly because of his pleasure in the animals they encountered and partly because Mrs Carney was the female equivalent of her spouse. Josef had never encountered anyone like her! Large, hearty, motherly and Cornish to the backbone, she immediately took him, quite literally, to her bosom.

'Well, my handsome, I've never seen such a pretty sight. Eyes like liquid pools, hasn't he, my love?'

Kate, watching Josef silently enjoy an enveloping hug, smiled shyly back at her, naturally finding no fault in such admiration of, and interest in her son.

This, she thought sadly, was exactly what Josef had missed. Being part of a loving family with grandparents to dote on him. How she wished she could have provided it for him.

The fragrance of the baking pasties filled the kitchen. First they were taken round to the stables and introduced to Delilah the horse, Sam the dog, and Jezebel the goat.

'There's no farming here as such.' Jim explained. 'Some years I sell Christmas trees and sometimes I fatten beef-stock, but we knew we were planning a trip this year and there's nothing like that at present. Still, there are plenty of young trees so you can use one for yourselves come Christmas.'

That was encouraging, Kate thought. It sounded as though he had made up his mind to let them stay!

When a tiny kitten was lifted, mewing and put into Josef's hands he clearly felt himself in paradise! He sat on the rug in the warm kitchen and played with his small, furry friend, totally absorbed, for a good hour.

The grown-ups talked and the pasties baked, and Kate lost some of her waif-like look as the tension escaped from her.

Anxious not to deceive them more than she had to, she told them. 'There is a reason I need to be away from anyone I know. It's nothing criminal. I just hope that — ' she broke off.

'You don't need to say any more.' Jim Carney had already made up his mind. 'I think we can get a pretty good idea of what you mean. These days, with so many broken relationships, girls like you, with children to take care of on their own all too often have a raw deal. As long as you feel capable of looking after the place and the animals, you're welcome to be here while we're away. Do you feel up to it?'

Kate looked at him gratefully, and slowly nodded her head. She said shakily, 'I need it so much. You look like a guardian angel to me. I can't believe you're willing to take a chance on us. I swear your trust won't be misplaced. I'll look after everything as though it were mine — more so.'

They had laughed, patted her on the shoulder and shown her the bedrooms for her and Josef.

'There's no need for you to go back to London, m'dear. We can be off in a few days and you can have a bit of a holiday getting used to things here.'

After that, with surprising efficiency, considering their sleepy appearance, the Carney's had swung into action, ringing airlines to confirm tickets, phoning their daughter about arrival times and making lists, both for Kate and themselves.

Later, after a protracted dinner, even Josef, who had managed nearly a whole pasty, was unable to find a corner for the fresh scones and thick, yellow cream Mrs Carney offered them.

'But I will later,' he assured her kindly, not wishing her to think him unappreciative or to miss any of the available treats! He had spotted a big, chocolate cake in the cool pantry when chasing after the fleeing kitten.

'So you will, my little brave,' she replied. 'Maybe for breakfast.'

She twinkled at the other adults. 'When you've had your bacon and scrambled eggs, of course.'

'Breakfast? Are we going to sleep here?'

Josef turned hopeful eyes to his mother and was rewarded with a smile and nod. He was so thrilled at this prospect that even being refused permission to share his bed with his new playmate was unable to damp his high spirits. Especially when he was gravely informed by Mr Carney that the first task in the morning was to decide on a name for the kitten . . .

★ ★ ★

Kate still found it hard to believe she was here on Dartmoor even though the Carney's had been gone for six weeks and bad weather had set in. She watched the snow falling, from the kitchen window, hoping that they would not be cut off from the village.

Perhaps it was some comfort that, with this soft, white blanket around them, no-one would creep up to the house unseen. Their footprints would shout their presence!

Since coming here, Kate had put on weight and begun enjoying life, but old habits of thinking die hard. She still watched, still had jumpy times. Today had been one of them.

She shivered. Please don't let them be out there. Don't let them be on her trail.

She hoped fervently that her instincts were wrong, that the anxious gut feeling she'd had all day was just a reaction to the banshee howling of the wind.

The snow had been falling all day. It would be drifting, she must shovel it away from the path between the house and the barn. For the first time, a doubt came as to whether she had done the right thing in coming to Dartmoor. Had she placed them in a web to wait for the spider?

Before leaving, Jim Carney had taken them to the village and introduced Kate to the vicar, the shopkeeper, and the publican. She had been friendly but distant, frightened of too much public knowledge of her presence. Perhaps that had been a mistake, it would be nice to have a friend locally now that winter was well and truly here!

'Mummy, Mummy, Sam wants a biscuit.' Giggling, Josef hurled himself into the kitchen, the curly, brown and white dog close behind him. Sam, missing his master, had attached himself to Josef and become his shadow. Kate knew that no companion more trustworthy or affectionate than the intelligent collie could have been found for him.

'Sam isn't the one begging for biscuits. It's Josef who wants biscuits.'

'Ooh, look it's all white.'

Josef, raised to window height stopped giggling, awed by the changing landscape outside. Thumb in mouth he relaxed against her. His dark curls tickled her neck and she said, 'It's snow, darling. Would you like to go out in it?'

At his vigorous nod, she said, 'We'll put on all your warm things — and your red wellies. Mummy has to clear a path so that she can see to the animals.'

Josef lifted his head. 'Sam, too?' he enquired anxiously.

'Yes, Sam, too.' She put him down. 'Go and get your bucket and spade.'

He dashed off, the dog bounding alongside and she heard him say importantly, 'It's snow, Sam, and we can play sand-castles.'

Once they were well muffled up, Kate, suspicious as always, went through the door first and stood looking around. No sign of human presence but the wind was definitely getting up. She'd have to hurry.

They strode through the clogging, soft whiteness, Kate swinging a hefty spade, Josef entranced at having to wade. Kate blessed the Carneys for having had the path paved. It shouldn't be too difficult to keep it cleared.

She had a struggle with the barn door even when she'd shovelled the snow away from it but it finally creaked open. Inside the solid wooden building the air was less icy. Even the creature's breath created some warmth.

Except for Jezebel's bleating requests to be milked and the soft nicker of the horse, it was church-like quiet out of the wind.

'Poor old Delilah.' Kate loved the slender, brown mare. 'Let's walk you up and down a bit.'

Later, with Delilah back in her stall

and the goat attended to, she returned to the open door. Already the path was covered with a relentless white carpet.

The nightmare thought came of an accident out here alone in these conditions. What would become of Josef?

'Stop being stupid,' she scolded herself out loud. 'We've got a phone and a car.' Not that the car would be much use in deep snow.

'What did you say, Mummy?' Josef came up, skidded and sat down, plump on his well-padded bottom.

'Nothing that matters. Come on.' She started building up the snow. 'Let's make a snowman.'

In another twenty minutes, with potatoes for eyes, a carrot for a nose and an old trilby of Jim Carney's to top it, they had, according to Josef, the best snowman in the whole world.

'How do you know?' Kate teased. 'You've never seen one before.'

'I've seen pictures,' he affirmed

stoutly, 'and our Mr Carney is the bestest.'

'Mr Carney? Oh, I see — because of the hat.' Kate laughed. 'I shouldn't think he'd be flattered. Anyway, we must go in now — before we freeze. A bath for you, I think — and hot chocolate for both of us.'

2

With the warmth of the central heating, coming indoors was like entering a haven. Kate sat Josef on the table, pulled off his things and chased him into the downstairs bathroom. Once he was happily ensconced in the warm bubbles and surrounded by bath toys, she set a match to the living-room fire. She must remember to keep up her stack of kindling!

The sky outside was leaden, both with heavy clouds and the march of darkness. Would the snow never stop? It had lost its prettiness now and was definitely ominous.

She switched on the yard light. Yellow brilliance flooded the re-whitened path and the sentinel snowman. He had become fatter already. Keeping an ear tuned for the chatty monologue and small splashings from the open

19

bathroom door Kate turned on the local TV news. An MP had things to say about the county roads, a prisoner had escaped from Princetown jail, a woman had won the Pools and the weather was expected to worsen.

'Worsen!' Kate exclaimed in horror. 'How can it worsen?'

The girl announced cheerfully that outlying districts on Dartmoor were cut off.

'If isolated farmers put a coloured blanket on their fields tomorrow it will be seen by search helicopters,' the announcer continued, 'and food or animal supplies can be dropped to them.'

Why not telephone, Kate thought, before realising that lines might be down. Quickly she went to hers and was rewarded with a reassuring dialling tone.

There was a sudden shriek from the bathroom. Josef had slipped on the soap. Unhurt in anything save his dignity, he was quickly restored to sunniness.

In pyjamas and dressing-gown he was as voluble as ever, enjoying a boiled egg and a banana before playing with Benjy, the kitten, in front of the fire. At bedtime he followed his mother unprotestingly upstairs. The snow had tired him out, she thought, as she read to him, for the umpteenth time, the tale of a bad rabbit! Long before she had finished, Josef's lashes were shading his cheeks.

Kate went downstairs. She was restless. Her sense of unease, the instinct that something threatened, had been gnawing at her all day. Not just the usual fear, something new. She tried to ignore it, cooked an omelette, read a magazine, but at nine o'clock she gave up. She would see another weather report then go outside to clear the path again.

Turning on the television brought only static. Even as she pressed the remote control, the set went dead. The electricity had failed! For a stunned moment after all the lights went out, Kate sat immobile. Then she sprang up.

She must think — and organise light and heat.

Josef would be frightened if he woke up and did not see the landing light on. Quickly, with trembling hands, she took matches and lit the oil lamp on the bureau. Then, holding it aloft, she went to a drawer in the kitchen where she knew she would find night-lights, candles and holders. She blessed Mrs Carney's foresightedness. Her shadow on the pale staircase wall was hugely black. Already the house was striking cold, now that the pump had stopped working. She put another coverlet over Josef and left a night-light on a saucer. Tonight she would sleep in here with him on the other bed.

Downstairs, she put a candle in each of the three principal rooms. It made getting about easier.

Sam, ears pricked, had begun to follow her about. She sat down again rubbing the dog's silky head.

'Well, old boy, we can't put it off any longer. Like it or not we've got to go out and see to the animals.'

He gave a short bark, signifying his intention of staying with her through thick and thin.

Her parka, gloves and woolly hat were behind the front door. On the way across the hall she passed a full-length mirror. In her jeans and fisherman's jersey she could have passed for a boy. Big, scared eyes stared back at her.

'Stop it,' she murmured realising that she was half expecting another face to appear in the shadows behind her —

Back in the kitchen she pulled on parka and boots.

'Come on, Sam, good boy.' She propped open the door and held her lamp high, before setting it down and beginning to scrape away again with her spade. It was hard work, but doing it made her feel less helpless, more in charge. When she reached the barn door and managed to haul it back, the darkness inside was tomb-like. She held up her lamp!

Seeing all the hay reminded her of the

need to be careful. The thought of starting a fire was enough to make her blood run cold.

Carefully, she hung up the lamp and set to work attending to the horse, talking softly as she moved round. Jezebel needed nothing — although insatiable, she had plenty of food.

It was a relief to finish the chores and know she would soon be cosily back indoors! Pulling the door shut behind her, she pushed the bolt in place — and was shaken rigid by a sudden shattering series of barks from Sam.

Standing stiffly beside her he was glaring, wild-eyed at the barn door. And, as the barks changed to a lips-drawn-back growl, she too heard what had set him off.

Not the familiar tap of Delilah's hooves, nor the bleat of Jezebel. These Sam would have recognised. No, this was different — a bump, drag, drag noise and, horrifyingly the sound of laboured breathing.

At first Kate was immobile with

horror. Then her thoughts began to race. Was it a man or an animal. Was it one of Sirius's men?

She put a hand on the dog's collar to quieten the threats he was making deep in his throat. Trying to keep her voice resolute she called, 'Who's there? What do you want?'

Instantly there was silence. Whoever was there seemed to be holding their breath. So was she, she found, as she let it go and softly exhaled.

'I'm going to fetch my husband,' she shouted. 'He'll be out with his gun.'

Then, holding Sam's collar, she made for the house. Turning her back was hard, she felt as though some nameless thing would burst out and pounce on her. Heedless now of semi-darkness, she hurtled into the kitchen and slammed the door behind her. Only then, when they were safely inside, did she give way to the shaking which had begun to vibrate her whole body.

She must ring the police — even though the track must be impossible.

On trembling legs she sped to the phone, but this time her earlier fears were realised. The line was dead. The storm had truly cut them off.

A moan escaped her lips. She had never felt so alone! Alone to protect Josef and deal with whatever unnamed presence lurked out there in the barn.

Remembering Josef she was galvanised into action. Everything was locked, but she must leave Sam on guard at the foot of the stairs. He would be their second defence after the locks. A pang smote her at the idea of anything hurting the faithful creature, but Josef came first.

She fetched Jim Carney's twelve bore gun. Loading and firing was beyond her, but she could at least pretend!

'Stay, Sam!' She shut the hall door so that he could only roam there.

Upstairs, she barricaded them in by tugging the dressing-table across the back of the bedroom door. Josef did not stir then, or later, when she stretched herself on the other bed and put the gun down beside her. Her third and fourth defence.

For a long time she lay tense and rigid, staring wide-eyed into the flickering shadows. The bedside clock ticked and Josef's breath was even.

Her ears were pricked, razor sharp for the sounds she dreaded. Footsteps, breaking glass, anything untoward. Nothing stirred, and slowly, as time went by, her muscles relaxed.

When her teeth chattered she slid quietly under the coverlet. The house in its blanket of snow remained silent. In the early hours of the morning Kate's eyelids dropped over her eyes and she slept . . .

'Mummy, Mummy.' Josef was tugging at her arm. Her head swam.

Josef, standing beside her was clearly intrigued at finding her in his room.

'What you doing, Mummy?' And then, with a wriggle he said, 'I want to go to the bathroom.'

'Oh, darling, of course, you must be freezing. Wait just a moment.'

Kate was fully awake now. Aching and stiff but awake. Daylight was flooding in. Hopefully she clicked the light switch but the power had not been restored.

There were things to do, but wherever Josef went, she must go first.

As she pulled back the dressing-table from the door she recognised its flimsiness. So much for her third defence!

Kate let Sam out into the yard. The thick snow showed no trace of any tracks other than her own. She turned on the gas oven and left the door open to spread the hot air, then put on a bowl of porridge. The kitten discovered the warmth and sat, paws neatly together raising its tiny face to enjoy it. Kate laughed at its expression of ecstasy and suddenly her night-time fears seemed nonsensical.

After she had made a good fire in the lounge she would leave Sam with Josef and go out to the animals. Probably it was a badger or a fox she had heard.

The barn door opened easily and Jezebel set up her usual cacophony. Delilah gave a whinny of welcome. Relief flooded through Kate. They were both all right.

Nonetheless, when she had seen to their comfort she began a cautious investigation. Something had made that noise. Leaving the door propped open she advanced into the recesses of the barn, holding the gun in her hands.

She found him in the very back where it was darkest. He was lying on a bed of straw behind some bales of hay and a spare blanket of Delilah's covered him. He was asleep.

Blood from a deep cut on his neck had seeped and blackened the collar of his jacket. Where his legs protruded from the blanket his denim jeans were cut and torn, exposing a gash on his left leg which looked angry and puffy.

Kate, wide-eyed, kept the gun pointed in case he woke up. Who was he? Why was he here? What would he do when he woke up?

His sleep was restless, he tossed and turned and murmured. She wondered if he could be suffering from exposure. Clearly he was in bad shape, possibly delirious — and his wounds badly needed attention.

She agonised over what she should do. If only the phone had been working — or if she could have taken Josef and gone for help in the car. As it was, she was alone with a difficult decision.

Quietly, she eased herself on to a bale of hay, the gun across her knees, and studied the stranger.

He was in his thirties, as dark as Josef and thin-faced. Several days of growth covered his chin but his mouth was a sweet curve and his eyebrows proudly arched. It's ridiculous, Kate thought, that a man in this condition could look aristocratic, but he did!

She surveyed his length. A tall man, over six feet. There were deep lines running from nose to mouth and a small frown line between his brows. The lines were too well etched to be new, so it would seem that this was a man who had suffered.

Oh, for goodness' sake, stop it, she told herself. What on earth was she thinking about, sitting assessing a stranger. Yet still she was conscious of a charisma about him even in sleep. What was she to do? Leaving was just not good enough. She would be forced to come out again and, for another thing, he looked capable of finding a way in.

His eyes flickered and a groan escaped his lips — the same sound she had heard through the door last night. It was a heartrending sound. Was he a fugitive? If so, she knew what it was to be a runaway, always looking over your shoulder for your pursuers. And there was no way she could let a sick man stay in the freezing barn for another night.

How ill was he, she wondered, moving closer until her face was only inches from his. His lashes were as long as Josef's.

Suddenly, shockingly, she was held by

each wrist in an astonishingly powerful grasp. His arms had shot out from under the horse blanket, pushed away the gun and taken her captive in a hold stronger than she would have believed him capable. His sinewy fingers were boring relentlessly into her flesh.

Apart from Kate's startled, 'Oh,' as it happened, neither of them spoke. His now fully-open eyes were alarmingly close to hers. Irrelevantly, she noticed that they were dark topaz.

'One scream and it'll be your last.' The words were menacing, but the voice and accent were that of an educated man. She was mesmerised, held, chest to chest, face to face, hip to hip, forced to lie on top of him as though in a strait jacket. Could she perhaps kick his injured leg enough to make him let go — or would that be an invitation to violence.

'Don't try it. You'd be sorry.' His lips, twisting cynically were close to hers.

'Try what?'

'Whatever crossed your mind. I know

a calculating look when I see one.'

Kate's brain had begun to race. Keep him talking. If you get to know an assailant it's hard for them to molest you.

'Nothing crossed my mind. Except to wonder how I could help you.'

The words were gasped out because she could not draw deep breaths with his body so fiercely pressed against her.

'Help me!' He gave a short, disbelieving laugh. 'The only help you'd give me would be to run for your life and get someone — with a loaded gun this time.'

So he had spotted the uselessness of the twelve-bore. Well, at least he didn't know she was alone here. Perhaps she could bluff him.

The expression in the topaz eyes had begun to change, as he studied her face. 'You're lovely,' he said abruptly and his grip shifted.

It was all Kate needed to break free. With a sudden galvanic movement she stamped hard on his injured leg and was on her feet again in a flash.

Looking wildly around for a weapon she found the gun and held it over her head by the barrel prepared to bring it down if he came after her.

He was clutching his leg and moaning. When he eventually raised his head still holding on to his leg, the ravaged face he turned up to her was filled with pain — and a strange vulnerability. No-one should look like that, Kate thought, but she forced back the pang of pity. There was too much at stake to let compassion intervene. As wary as a mouse watching a cat she kept her eyes on him. Would he jump her? Would he exact revenge?

For a long time he gazed at the wild-eyed girl, as the agony — and anger — receded from his eyes.

At last he said, in a deep voice, 'Put it down. I'm not going to hurt you.'

He sounded subdued, beaten, at the end of his tether, but she could not afford to believe him. She kept the gun raised, watching for any sudden movements.

Nonetheless, when he said, 'Will you help me?' she nodded.

'I'm going to try and stand up now,' he said softly, 'Don't be afraid.'

She backed away a little and watched him wincingly get to his feet. Her assessment had been right, he was over six feet tall. In the barn's half-light he loomed over her.

'I'm giving up. Do what you want. Either we stay here or fetch someone or go to your house together.'

He tried to smile and she discovered that even a pain-wracked smile through several days growth of beard could be attractive. Some gut feeling, some primeval female instinct within her was beginning to trust him.

'I know the options as well as you. You need shelter and those wounds attended to. We had better — '

The speech was never finished. As she watched, her eyes locked on his face, his eyes slid away from her and became totally unfocused, as he folded his length at her feet. He had fainted!

Turning, Kate ran back to the house. How long, she wondered, could she rely on his being unconscious?

3

In the living-room, Josef and Sam were playing Snakes and Ladders, Josef kindly moving Sam's counters for him. She stroked the dog's silky head fondly. 'You're the finest baby-sitter in the world.'

Then, with fresh logs on the fire she re-secured the guard and left them again. What should she do? Wait for the injured man to turn up here — or go back and do what she could for him.

Waiting for something to happen made her feel like a victim. Better that she took the initiative, she decided. It was going to take courage though. She could only hope that her assessment of his character was the right one.

First she made a Thermos of hot coffee, fetched some blankets, and filled a hot water bottle. Warming him was the main consideration, but he needed food, too, so she made some sandwiches.

Perhaps, a hopeful little voice in her head said, by the time she returned, he would have disappeared!

Slipping and sliding back to the barn, she wondered if she were mad, but in common humanity what could she do? Let him die?

He was conscious and had propped himself up against the bale, but he looked dreadful, ashen-faced and limp, as though he had lost contact with the world. Even so, his eyes flew open at her entrance and a surprised look flickered across his face.

'You've come back.'

His dull gaze took in the blanket, tray and hot water bottle — and lingered on the food.

When Kate handed him the hot water bottle he took it and hugged it to him, quickly suppressing the involuntary groan of pure pleasure that escaped him.

Kate shook a blanket over him and said in nurse-like tones, 'Lift up your head please, for me to slide this pillow under it.'

When her face was close to his, he said, 'Why? Why not let me die?'

'Don't think for one moment that I didn't consider it. Just say that I'm an idiot — or that I was afraid you wouldn't die — or would take too long about it. I decided it was better if I kept my eye on you.'

He gave an appreciative bark of laughter, but was no longer really interested in anything except the sandwiches! He eyed them hungrily but, to her surprise, did not attempt to take one. Neither did he pick up the steaming mug of coffee she had placed beside him.

For a moment Kate did not comprehend the mixture of longing and anxiety with which he stared at them. Then she did and was angry. How dare he!

Brusquely she said, 'I didn't mean that I wanted to cause your death. There's no weedkiller in anything. Do you want me to taste it first?'

He reached forward and snatched a sandwich. Indistinctly he mumbled, 'What does it matter? I'm done for anyway.'

'A couple of wounds and a few days chill and hunger aren't going to finish you off,' Kate said impatiently.

The first two mouthfuls were devoured wolfishly, unheeding of his audience, but after that he looked at her shamefacedly before holding his hands round the mug, closing his eyes and letting the steam warm his face. Kate was reminded of something. Oh, yes, the kitten enjoying the heat of the gas oven.

He sipped the hot drink and lowered the mug again. Then he took a careful bite from a sandwich, put it down and chewed slowly. Kate shook her head in wonder. What kind of man was it, who, even when starving, still cared about good manners?

Presently she noticed that he had begun to have difficulty in swallowing because of the motion of his jaw against the neck wound. And when he had finished he leaned his head back on the pillow and let his eyelids drop.

'What now?' he asked wearily. 'Have you rung the police?'

'No.'

His eyes came open but he didn't look at her.

'Why not?'

'That's my business. I have a proposition to put to you.'

At this he turned his head and looked at her. 'A proposition? Are you sure you've got the right man?'

'No, I'm not sure who I've got,' Kate admitted honestly. 'But my guess is that you've escaped from the prison. The working parties I've seen in the village wore those denims. Nonetheless, I'm prepared to take you in, give you shelter, and dress those wounds until you're better. Then you can go — just disappear. On condition I have your solemn promise not to harm me, or my family.'

He was watching her closely and she

wondered if he could see through her, would guess that she was alone and cut off from the rest of the world.

Unexpectedly, he said softly, 'Do you have a name?'

'Of course I have a name. It's Kate. Never mind that, though, I want an answer. Do you accept my terms?'

'Sweet Kate.' Incredibly he was laughing, putting back his head, ignoring the wound on his neck. 'Bring me my contract, Kate, so that I can sign on the dotted line. Of course I accept your terms. It seems a small price. I'm hardly likely to get a better offer.'

She was incensed. How could this lean, dark, mystery man, caught in a trap as he was, laugh and mock in the face of his troubles? She couldn't understand such a mentality.

Kate had learned her lessons in a hard school. Losing both her parents, a marriage that was a nightmare and the years since filled with fear. She found nothing to laugh at in the situation they were in — and neither, she thought, should he!

He had sobered up and was looking at her thoughtfully. Now he said, abruptly, 'Standing there so small telling me I've got to agree to your terms. Don't you know I could break your neck with my two hands.'

The fear flooded back but Kate pushed it away and answered spiritedly, 'It's your neck that's close to being broken, not mine.'

He had seen the flash of fear and was quick to reassure her.

'I'm not going to hurt you, I promise.'

She had planned her story now, and began on it, feeling her way.

'My brother, with whom I live, doesn't want to know about this. It's his house, but he won't give you away. He's agreed to let me help you — but he doesn't want to meet you.'

'I see.'

The stranger's tone was neutral. Kate hoped that he didn't see at all, but it was the best she could do.

'Who else is in the house?' he asked.

She was suspicious. 'Why do you want to know?' She wondered whether to invent a husband but two invisible men were even more unlikely than one. 'Anyway there's only my son. He's just four and I'm going to try and get you in without his knowing.'

'You have a son?' the topaz eyes were definitely startled. 'You don't look old enough. Where's your husband?'

'I'm twenty-six if you must know — and my husband is — abroad. Can we stop wasting time? Are you strong enough to walk by yourself?'

'Of course I am.'

He pushed aside the blanket and got on to his knees, grimacing with the pain from his injured leg.

Fearing another faint, Kate said briskly, 'No, you're not. I'll take the things in and come back for you.'

She sped back to the house as fast as the glittering path would let her. With the daytime temperature so low it would freeze again tonight, she thought grimly. She made up the day bed in Jim's study.

The room had a fireplace and was next to the downstairs bathroom.

After a few minutes with Josef and once more building up the living-room fire, she steeled herself to go out again.

He was still leaning against the bale where he had fallen back and was almost as pale as the snow. She wondered how much blood he had lost. If he fainted on the way back, he would be too heavy for her to drag.

Wordlessly she handed him an old anorak of Jim Carney's. Those mobile eyebrows shot up again.

'What a generous brother you have,' he commented with heavy sarcasm.

'Put it on.'

'Yes, ma'am.' An attempt at a salute, a reaction to the hectoring way she had spoken. Kate was again impatient at his flippancy.

The anorak was far too roomy, but it would serve. Once he had got to his feet, Kate positioned herself in the fold of his good arm, drawing it over her shoulder.

'Lean on me, it isn't far to the house, you'll be fine.'

'Indeed I shall, with such a beast of burden. We must look rather mis-matched, but you fit very well in there, sweet Kate.'

She would have liked to fire up, to protest at the ridiculous name he had started using, but there was neither time nor breath. It was taking all her concentration to keep him moving.

At first he leaned only lightly on her but, as they progressed, his weight became an almost intolerable burden.

Later she would recall that walk from the barn as a nightmare, fearful all the way that his legs would buckle and he would pull her down.

His rasping breath grew louder and when they reached the kitchen he sank on to a chair.

'Let me rest — a minute.'

His head dropped on to his arms. Tensely she waited, afraid Josef would hear them and come to find her.

'Please come on, it's only a bit farther.'

She was nearly dancing with impatience, but when he raised his head, his gaunt expression alarmed her.

'I don't think I can manage stairs.'

'No, no, you don't have to,' she said soothingly, 'there's a bed downstairs ready — in my brother's study. Just a few more steps.'

He nodded, gave her a travesty of a smile and struggled to stand, visibly gritting his teeth. She slid once more under his arm and in five more minutes he was stretched full length on the bed she had prepared. Leaving him she hurried away. There were a million things to do — check on Josef, the animals, warm the kitchen, make some soup. For a while she would leave him alone to recover from that horrendous walk.

After a momentary hesitation, she turned the key on the outside of the study door. The last thing she wanted was for Josef to stumble upon her secret.

After all the teaching and lectures she had given him on never trusting strangers, how ironic that she should be the one who had introduced this volatile and dangerous element into their lives!

It was an hour before Kate was able to return to the study. To her relief, Josef, after a belated lunch, consented to a nap on the living-room couch. When she finally tiptoed softly back into the study, the mysterious stranger was asleep, too, his high cheek-bones even more prominent against his pallor. At some time he had removed his jacket and jeans and they were in a heap on the floor. She wondered fleetingly if he were naked. It made no difference, prudishness would have to be overcome if she were to dress his leg.

Not until the sparks and flames of a wood fire were sputtering up the chimney did she sit back and open the first aid box she had brought. It was well-stocked — bandages, scissors, antiseptic — everything she could possibly need. More of the Carney's foresight, she thought, smiling.

'What are you finding to smile about, Kate?'

She whirled about. 'I thought you were sleeping.'

'I was. That fire is a sight for sore eyes. May I come and warm myself.'

He moved as though to get up.

'No you can't.' Kate was vehement, still not sure if he had anything on and not anxious as yet to find out. 'You're to lie there and not move. I'm going to wash those wounds.'

'What a tyrant you are,' he responded, but he lay back docilely enough.

Kate went to the bed and he said apologetically, 'I'm afraid there may be some blood on your bedclothes. Not much. I'd done most of my bleeding already.'

'It doesn't matter.'

She considered asking him how he had got the gashes but decided it could wait. Laying pyjamas and dressing-gown on the bed she said, not meeting his eyes, 'these are my brother's.'

'Thank you.' He was being uncharacteristically meek! She hoped the clothes had convinced him that she really did have a resident brother.

'There's a bathroom right next door — only cold water, I'm afraid. The power is off. I've got hot water in the kitchen and I'll be back in a little while to bathe those wounds. Can you manage?'

'Of course.'

'You said that before — when we left the barn — and you couldn't,' she reminded him.

He laughed. 'I'm rested — and warm. I can wash and dress myself.'

But his eyes looked like hollow coals as they followed her to the door. She turned with her hand on the doorknob and said, 'Don't go anywhere else. The dog is in the sitting-room. My brother is upstairs.'

This time, when he spoke, there was no trace of flippancy. In fact, his tone was stern. 'I made a promise not to hurt you or yours. I intend to keep it. Take my word for it.'

The word of an escaped convict! Was she a fool to believe that she could trust him?

Once again she got busy, boiling water, collecting clothes, and when she finally returned he was sitting by the fire warming his hands, and wearing Jim's sedate, green pyjamas and towelling robe. He looked up, eyeing her preparations uneasily.

'Dr Livingstone, I presume?'

The flip side was back, was it, Kate thought, less impatient now because she knew he was apprehensive and trying to cover it up. Like Josef! When she'd put a plaster on his knee he'd said, 'It doesn't hurt, Mummy. My eyes are just watering.'

Men and boys, she thought, all afraid to lose face.

'How do you like the outfit?' he asked

with a look down at himself. 'Your brother is a big man — though not a snappy dresser.'

Perhaps her 'brother' had better have a name.

'Tom is a bit old-fashioned.' She said it primly avoiding his look.

'Tom?' he queried with the slanting eyebrows ever so slightly raised.

That couldn't possibly be a flicker of amusement could it?

Kate began laying out the things she would need. 'Yes, his name is Tom. And talking of names, isn't it about time I knew yours?'

He didn't answer for so long that she looked up questioningly. Seeing his shuttered face, she said quickly, 'It doesn't matter — you don't have to tell me.'

'Forgive me for hesitating, I realise that that's the least I owe you. My name is Max Heinemann.'

He watched her closely and she was aware of the tension emanating from him. When it was clear that his name meant nothing to her, his body relaxed slightly.

Kate continued, outwardly tranquil, with her preparations but she was alert and wondering. Had he been famous? She could imagine him as a well-known musician, artist or author. Maybe a tycoon — who had turned to embezzlement. He even seemed right for a jewel thief — the kind who laughed in the face of danger and eluded the authorities. Her imagination was running away with her. She must remember that, far from eluding the police, he had been well and truly caught.

'How do you do, Mr Heinemann.'

She was demure, unconsciously coquettish, looking up at him from her kneeling position and they both smiled. The formality sounded so absurd in that setting. He said gravely 'How do you do Mrs — er — '

'Lennox,' she supplied hastily, 'and I'm ready now. Take off the pyjamas and lie on the bed please.'

Obediently he limped to the bed and

stretched his long body on it, asking, with an air of false modesty 'Can't I just roll them up?'

'No.' Kate was firm. 'That gash is too high. The towelling robe will cover your — blushes.'

She turned to pick up a towel to lay under the leg and when she went back to the bed he was ready.

Kate tried her hardest not to hurt him, but the next fifteen minutes could not be other than difficult for both of them. The wound would fester further unless she got all of the dirt out of it and she was determined to do a good job.

At one point she said distractedly, 'It ought to be stitched.'

'Don't be ridiculous.' The pain-wracked voice was harsh. He had not moved under her probing but had spent the time looking steadfastly at the ceiling. 'You know as well as I do, that's impossible. Scarring won't bother me.'

She said no more until a reluctant groan was dragged from him.

'I'm sorry. I can't help it.'

He brought his gaze down from the ceiling. In a voice that was almost a growl he said, 'I know. Get on with it. Do what you have to.'

Only when the final bandage had been tied did the coiled-spring tension leave him. Kate sent up a prayer of thanks that it was over, and her patient lay back, eyes closed and breath shallow. She let him rest, as she cleared up the things, wondering how she could possibly put him through the agony of enduring her ministrations to the wound on his neck.

'Kate.'

She looked up to find him half-sitting up, looking down at his leg.

'Yes?'

'Thanks. I know that was hard for you. It looks and feels like a good job. Are you a doctor?

'No. But I trained as a nurse. Only I got married and went to live abroad before I took my finals.'

'Oh — well, thanks. I'm grateful.' He

leaned wearily back.

'I'm going to leave you now, to get a meal for my son — and brother. I'll bring you some, too — but I won't be back until this evening.'

The face he turned towards her was haunted and bleak. A stab of pity went through Kate. She said gently, 'I wish I had something to give you for the pain.'

He held out a hand in a gesture as innocent as a child reaching for its mother. When Kate put hers into it, the clasp was surprisingly strong.

'You've been incredible,' he said. 'I only wish we could have met under different circumstances, and don't worry about the next session. I'll grit my teeth and bear it. Thanks, sweet Kate.'

She had to remind herself fiercely that here, in front of her, charming and vulnerable though he was, was an escaped convict.

'I didn't have much choice,' she said shortly. 'I could hardly let you die.'

'I'm sure you're much too humane for that.'

He let her hand go and Kate went to the door. As she shut it behind her, she saw that his eyes were already closed.

4

It was nine o'clock that evening before Kate dressed Max Heinemann's neck wound. In spite of having to do it by candlelight, the experience was not nearly as harrowing as attending to his leg had been, earlier in the day.

The improvement was chiefly because she had made the decision to give him not only a large shot of Jim's whisky, but other, even more effective things as well! Things about which she had not consulted him, but still known only a small pang of conscience, as she gave them to him!

After the second glass of whisky he looked at her over the rim and said, a little muzzily, 'Is this the anaesthetic you wanted to give me this afternoon?'

Kate discovered that she was unable to lie. Strange, she thought, here have I been living a lie for years, yet one direct question from this man and the truth comes bubbling to the surface.

'Partly it is. Alcohol dulls the senses. I didn't mean to tell you, but I've also crushed a couple of pain-killers and sleeping pills into the food you ate. They should take effect quite soon. I only wish I'd thought of it before I did your leg.'

For one single moment he looked murderous, then, after a glance at her face, he burst out laughing.

'You're an amazing woman. Honestly! You look about as strong as a sparrow, but you've got the resolution of a — a she bear. I've got a pathological hatred of putting my fate in somebody else's hands, but it seems you've got me entirely in the palm of your hand — by fair means or foul. For better or worse then, Kate. Try not to do your worst because obviously I don't have any say in the matter.'

Exuding a confidence she did not feel, Kate said tranquilly, 'Thanks. I was afraid you might not like it — that's why

I didn't consult you. Knocking you out any other way was beyond my capabilities and it seemed the best thing to do. And, incidentally, I'm not too keen on being likened to a bear — or a sparrow come to that.'

She was biding her time, waiting for the right moment, when his senses should begin to slide away.

Had he, she wondered, noticed that she'd changed her clothes, discarded grubby jeans in favour of black trousers and cowl-necked, turquoise sweater?

Upstairs, after putting Josef to bed, she'd slipped a pair of opal earrings into her ears, telling herself sternly that she was just making an effort to keep up her morale. There was no question of trying to impress — anyone!

Now, she slipped on an oversized apron belonging to Mrs Carney.

Max watched her with a slightly detached eye, as though her preparations were nothing to do with him, but she knew he was still aware.

He said, slurring the words slightly,

'Blue eyes, earrings and sweater. You ought to be a blonde.'

Kate, who was a natural blonde until she'd dyed her hair jet black as part of her effort to elude Sirius, tried not to laugh. No question about whether he would be fit enough to notice anything different she thought! He hadn't missed a thing!

Thank goodness though, that all the stuff she'd given him was beginning to take effect. His muscles were becoming slacker and more relaxed. When he spoke he was even slipping into the maudlin.

'S'pose you want to make me drunk, sweet Kate. Take care! Only have yourself to blame if I got amorous with you.'

'Don't talk like that, I don't like it.' She was as severe as a head nurse.

'Anyway, I don't have anything to worry about,' she added hastily, remembering her imaginary protector. 'You know I only have to call my brother.'

'Tom, the brother,' Max announced

happily, smiling rather vacuously and appearing pleased with himself for remembering the name.

She was feeling amazingly unruffled considering what lay ahead, quietly certain, at the moment, of her ability to keep him in check, but wishing he would succumb completely to the potent brew he had imbibed.

Hopefully he held out the empty glass for a refill, and she said firmly, 'No, that's the last drink. I don't want you thrashing about at the wrong moment.'

He gazed at her owlishly, before saying with a distinct air of provocation 'Well, you could always ask your brother in to hold me still, couldn't you.'

There it was again, the innuendo. Did he suspect? She managed to keep her serene front.

'I could but I'm not going to. I told you he wants to keep out of this.'

'Oh, yes, I forgot.'

Definitely sceptical, she thought, illogically annoyed that he seemed not to believe her.

'I didn't used to get drunk on two glasses' he said, a little shamefacedly, 'Just haven't had any for three years.'

Kate was silent. So he had been in jail for three years had he? That would have been the time when she was bringing Josef back to England and certainly would have had little interest in any newspaper reported court cases.

She judged it wiser to say no more, guessing that he had reached a stage where it was time for her to get busy. It was incredible that he was still talking after what she had given him; he must have a strong constitution in spite of his haggard look.

'Lie down,' she commanded. 'And stop talking.'

He put down the glass with an unsteady hand.

'You're a tyrant, Kate,' he slurred, but drowsiness had made him docile and he did as she told him.

Within moments his eyelids closed and, although he muttered something and attempted to rear up, her stillness was soon rewarded by gentle snoring.

Good! At long last her 'cocktail' had worked. Now she could get on with the business of cleaning his wound — and this time, she vowed to herself — she would stitch it. Deftly and speedily she worked in peace, conscious of no sound except the crackle of the fire in the grate and the stertorous breathing of the man on the bed.

* ★ *

Hours later, Josef, though still half-asleep, spoke to her as she crept softly into his room.

'You going to sleep with me again, Mummy?'

'Darling, you shouldn't be awake still.' Kate, having completed all her chores, was nearly dropping from exhaustion. 'Is that night light bothering your eyes?' she enquired. 'Or are you too chilled to sleep well?'

'No, it's all right. My bed's nice and warm, I just woke up when you came in.' Josef yawned mightily. He was obviously not going to stay awake long.

Tiredly, Kate bent to kiss him and told him, 'Go back to sleep, now. I'll still be here in the morning.'

'Have you got the gun?' he asked sleepily.

'Gun?'

For a moment she was at a loss, before recalling that she had kept it beside her on the previous night. Was it really only last night? Her day had been so packed with drama and incident that it seemed decades ago.

'No, Josef, I haven't got the gun. Good-night, sweetheart.'

'Good-night, Mummy.'

As she climbed into the other bed, Kate felt as though she were the only one still awake in the whole world. At least in her little world! All were asleep! The animals in the barn, Sam and Benjy down by the embers of the living-room fire, Josef, here beside her and Max Heinemann in the study.

'Max.' She whispered his name

experimentally into the semi-darkness, savouring it on her lips. It was not a soft name. There was a hard abrupt sound to it. She wondered if it were short for something — Maxwell or Maximillian, perhaps. What a mouthful that would be!

Who was he, she wondered, this mysterious, dark, enigma. All she really knew about him was that he was a convicted criminal and desperate enough to escape in the depths of winter. Not very reassuring that! The odd thing was that he had expected her to recognise his name — and been relieved when she didn't.

What else did she know about him? That he was courageous, mocking his own pain and fears. That he had a lot of anger in him, especially frightening when it erupted.

Most of all, though, despite his present vulnerability she knew that he was strong. Strong! Nonsense, how could she possibly know that, said her other more sceptical self. It was instinct, not knowledge, that told her that — and her instinct had been proved wrong once before. She must be careful.

Nonetheless, her last waking thought was a surprised wonder that tonight, still in the depths of a star-shrouded farm on Dartmoor without telephone or electricity, she felt none of the fears associated with the previous night. Instead she snuggled down into the little bed and fell asleep, filled with a sense of being protected, no longer being alone — a feeling that even Kate herself recognised as being thoroughly unrealistic!

When she woke it was with a start and a moment of chilled fear. Had she been dreaming? It certainly wasn't morning yet, no daylight penetrated the curtains. There was a nightmarish quality about her waking, like the hangover from a fearsome dream.

Her now wide open eyes gazed into the blackness, gradually adjusting. The night light, though low, was still providing a beam of luminosity. Shapes began to appear. The outlines of the furniture, the wall-mirror, Josef's bed, the child soundlessly asleep under the coverlet. Her watch, held close to her face told her it was half past four.

Something must have woken her. The door was ajar. Ajar! A leap of memory came. She had shut it when she came to bed. And yes, her straining ears caught a faint sound from the corridor, even though it was carpeted.

Soft footsteps! She was sure of it. Someone was moving about, going in and out of the rooms. Someone had been in here and it was his leaving that had woken her.

That someone could be none other than Max Heinemann. How long, she wondered angrily, had he stood and looked at them, she and Josef, defence-lessly, unknowingly asleep?

Now he was undoubtedly investigating the house, looking, she supposed, for her 'brother,' sizing up the situation he was in, guarding his back.

Like any other cornered rat, she

thought scornfully.

At first her brain, with the dreamlike fear still hanging over her, was sluggish, but reason began slowly to reassert itself. Since he had been in here and gone away again, they were in no immediate danger — if they had been in any at all.

No, he would not harm her, she could be sure of that. Not only because he had cause to be grateful to her but because, in his weakened state he was still largely dependent on her for his welfare.

A still, small voice in her head cried, 'What about when he is better? What will he do then?'

She put that thought aside for the present. Shock and fright had been replaced by resentment — even fury. She had, whatever her motives, saved his life, done an awful lot for him, much of which had cost her dear. And this was how he repaid her! By not believing her, by searching the house for himself, checking on her. Damn him, why could he not have trusted her. After all, she had not lied to him — except about the phone and having a man in the house — and surely they were understandable shadings given the circumstances.

Moving quietly, so as not to wake Josef, she slipped on her dressing-gown and tiptoed into the corridor flattening herself against the wall. She would confront him presently but first she would see what he was up to, make sure that he was simply snooping.

The thought that he was looking for something valuable to steal crossed her mind with distaste. Somehow that was unbearable. Unconsciously she had begun to feel she knew him, and a common thief was not compatible with the man she believed him to be. But he had to have been jailed for something, the sceptical side said. Would fraud or embezzlement be any better than burglary?

In the corridor her eyes had to adjust again to almost complete darkness, but there was a faint lightening over the stair well. It looked as though he had done with his tour of the upper level and had gone down again into the hall.

Bare feet making no sound on the carpet, she tiptoed to the top of the banisters and looked over. The hall was empty but the living-room door was open and inside she could hear a low voice.

'Hello, old boy. No, down now, don't make a noise, you're a fine fellow, aren't you.'

Sam didn't even bark but, to her chagrin, Kate could hear a happy panting and shuffling, the sound the dog made when greeting a friend.

Oh, but it was maddening! Another of her defences down, another of her protective falsehoods exposed. The fierce dog was shown up as the friendliest creature one could find.

A sense of forlorn defencelessness came over her as she stood shivering at the top of the stairs. This man, after all he had been through, and all he had swallowed, should have been deeply asleep for the rest of the night. Instead he was creeping about her house, stripping away all the fragile little barriers with which she had surrounded herself. How could she ever have been so stupid as to feel glad that Max Heinemann was in the house before she had dropped off to sleep — and woken to the grim reality that he was a dangerous intruder.

What a fool she was — what a susceptible fool! She had actually liked him, actually been drawn to him, found him interesting. But no-one, not even the naïve idiot she had turned out to be would be anything but suspicious of this fugitive who was furtively searching the house in such an underhand way.

Max came out into the hall again and Kate pressed herself back against the wall in the shadows, unwilling to let him see her.

The candle he was holding showed him, serious-faced, dark-visaged and intent. She realised, as she watched him, that it was the limp she had heard. It was hard to move quietly when you were dragging one foot.

With the whiteness of his bandaged neck, his midnight-black mane of hair and scruffy growth of beard, he looked incredibly menacing. Even incongruously dressed, as he was, in Jim's towelling robe!

She had meant to confront him, but now a craven fear, a reluctance to face him, made her hesitate. He was looking for something. With the candle held high, he was turning, scanning the hall. Kate held her breath and tried to keep perfectly still. After a moment's scrutiny he found what he was after. With a sinking heart she realised what it was! The telephone! A small, 'Ah!' of satisfaction escaped him as he saw what he was searching for. He shuffled to pick it up, putting the candle down on the bureau beside him.

Despair again gripped Kate as he held it to his ear for a moment and then put it back on it's cradle. Now he knew that it was not humanity which had prevented her calling the police. What would he do now that he knew it all!

She saw his face as he picked the candle up again. His eyebrows were together in the ominous frown that must have caused those permanent lines there and his mouth was shut tight, the lips pressed together.

She thought aggrievedly that he should be pleased to know that there was no communication between them and the rest of the world. Instead he was clearly rigid with fury!

This time, instead of holding the candlestick at shoulder level as he had done previously he lifted it high, high enough to illuminate the stairs and landing.

Instantly Kate knew that he had seen her.

His voice, when he spoke, was low but his tone was immeasurably sarcastic. 'I'll fetch my brother from the house, he'll come out with a gun. I'll set the dog on you. My brother is in the house, I only have to call. Oh, no I haven't rung the police, I only want to help you.'

He was quoting the things she had said — quoting them with malice and barely suppressed rage! What should she do? Silently, as though she had not heard him, she stood, holding her blue, velvet dressing-gown to her and did not move a muscle. She was aware that he was filled with fury, as volatile as a powder keg. Light the blue touch paper and retire.

I must not do anything to inflame him, she thought. Remembered fears returned to haunt her. All too clearly could she recall Sirius whipping himself up to a frenzy before he hit out.

'Empty threats, Kate, empty threats, and false kindness.' Max almost spat out the words, louder this time.

She was galvanised into whispering fiercely 'Please! Don't make so much noise. I don't want to wake Josef.'

He seemed to grow temporarily calmer. 'No. At least the son was true.'

The face he turned up to her was blue-shadowed with tiredness. Seeing the tiredness, Kate hoped the sleeping pills were still working and that soon he would want only to sleep once more. But he only took a deep breath and seemed to be controlling himself with an iron grip.

'Come down. I want to talk to you.'

She didn't move. 'Wouldn't it be better if we waited until the morning?'

'No.' It was a flat negative and it did not brook refusal. If she had hoped to placate him until he was calmer the hope died.

Again she was aware of his suppressed rage and believed she must obey. Trying to maintain her dignity in spite of bare feet, she came down the stairs and went past him into the living-room.

Sam was delighted to have company again and frisked around her. Max, coming in behind her, put the candle on a table and bent to throw a log on to the fire.

Sitting up very straight on the corner of the couch Kate said, 'You seem to be making yourself very much at home in my house. I thought I asked you to stay in the study.'

'So you did.' He said it with deliberate unpleasantness, baiting her. 'But then you said a lot of things, my not-so-sweet Kate. I should have known, shouldn't I, that there was no truth in you.'

He leaned forward and stared into her eyes, his own topaz ones darkly resentful.

'It wasn't kindness that made you look after me. You had no choice, did you? Other than letting me die. And I was beginning to think you some sort of angel. You're just like every other woman. They always let you down.'

He put a world of loathing in the words and Kate, to her own horror, wanted suddenly to cry — or to cry out in her own defence.

She was furious with herself, and with the wave of weakness and emotion that had triggered off her near bout of tears. It cost her an effort to overcome it but she was determined he shouldn't have the satisfaction of seeing how much his diatribe had affected her.

Looking straight at her tormentor Kate raised her chin in the unconscious gesture that showed she was not defeated.

Crisply, keeping her voice steady, she said, 'What did you expect? Should I have taken you on trust?'

'Trust!' He seemed to be trying the word for size as though he had never heard it before, but there was an arrested look on his face. 'No, don't trust anyone, Kate.' He gave a mirthless laugh. 'Least of all me.'

His hard eyes ran over her, her dark hair, her tense face, and came to rest on the slight body outlined by the dressing-gown.

Kate, suddenly fearful of where such an angry scrutiny might lead, licked her lips nervously and held the edges together more tightly.

'Oh, don't worry.' He was immediately aware of what she was thinking and contemptuously scornful. 'I may be a convicted criminal, but I never had to stoop to rape.'

There was an uncomfortable silence for a second and then he said, as though the words were wrenched out of him, 'Did my name really mean nothing to you?'

At her emphatic head-shake of denial, he said, 'If you're telling me the truth, where were you four years ago?'

'I was abroad — out East — for over a year.'

At his look of disbelief, she added, 'I was married — to Josef's father — and I didn't return until Josef was one.'

'I see.'

He looked as if he wanted to ask more about that but instead said slowly, 'So you really didn't know. Then I'd better tell you why I was in prison.'

He got up and limped to the fireplace, too restless to sit down any longer. Picking up the poker he jabbed at a blazing log.

'It was hot news at the time. I made

all the front pages.'

He laughed jeeringly, more, she decided, at himself than at her.

'You were quite right to be afraid of me, Kate. I didn't go to prison for stealing a necklace or fiddling my tax returns. I was there for the big one. I was jailed for murder. The murder of my wife.'

Kate paled. His words seemed to hang in the air between them like a visible curse. For a full minute, she was shocked into dumb immobility then her brain began to race. Without even knowing that she did it, she recoiled from him.

When he saw her shrink back it seemed to inflame him further.

He said, in a voice that was flat with venom and a wish to hurt, 'See, Kate, I was right, wasn't I? You must never trust anyone. They're all out to get you. What a little fool you've been, haven't you?'

Mutely, her eyes still fixed on the poker he was holding, she stood up.

A murderer, he was a murderer, a

murderer! The words seemed to be going round and round in her head.

Like a man possessed, as indeed he was, he brandished the poker.

'Hasn't it occurred to you that I could kill you here and now and nobody would be any the wiser?'

The angry voice seemed to bore into her brain. The hectoring harshness of him reminded her forcibly of Sirius just before he began hitting her.

Suddenly, she wanted nothing so much as to escape from him, from it, from the whole impossible horrible situation.

Putting both hands over her ears in a gesture of despair, she tried to shut it out, but it was useless. Max had not finished with her yet.

Dropping the poker, he brought his own hands up to hers and dragged them away from her head, hissing at her furiously, 'You're a fool — a stupid fool of a girl — to trust me or anyone.'

Kate could stand no more. Gasping, she jerked herself away from the vicinity of that grating, angry voice.

'Stop it!' she shrieked, heedless now of the noise they were making, 'Stop it, stop it, stop it.'

His grip loosened sufficiently for her to tear away. Hardly knowing what she was doing, she pulled her velvet wrap more tightly around her and ran headlong from the room. All the way up the stairs and along the corridor to the bedroom, she was whimpering with distress. Once she stumbled and fell, picking herself up and going on without even checking to see that she was all right. All that filled her mind was the horror of what she had just heard.

Dear God, what had she done? How could she have been so blind, so wrong, so idiotically sure that her instincts were right?

Just because Max Heinemann could be — in some moods — appealing, she had forgotten the precepts by which she had lived for the last three years.

Staying aloof from people, keeping her guard up, being suspicious of everyone, those were the rules which had kept her and Josef safe.

Until now!

Now was different!

Because she had done the unforgivable! She had let a murderer into the house. She had brought him in and ministered to his needs. She had brought him in where she and her son were alone, unprotected and virtually incapable of preventing a malicious killer from doing whatever he wished with them.

The man downstairs was not only aggressive, he was eaten up with anger and potentially violent. And she, choosing arrogantly to believe otherwise, had placed them in his power.

What kind of mother was she, she thought, with a twist of the heart, that she could endanger her child because she found a man attractive?

5

In the morning, it was a heavy-eyed Kate who took Josef's hand, and told him not to go rushing downstairs before she was ready to take him down. He blinked, but was docile enough, waiting impatiently for her, and seeming unaware of her strung up tension.

As they went down the stairs, Sam skittered up to them, emitted short welcoming barks and waving his fringed tail.

Kate shushed him fretfully, she had had wild hopes of getting out of the house and away before Max Heinemann woke.

Josef immediately entered into one of his 'conversations' with the collie and knelt to stroke and cuddle him.

'We'll go out today, shall we, Sam? And slide down the hill on the snow. You'd like to be tied up to a sledge thing, wouldn't you? Mummy, Sam wants to be a husky dog — like the Eskimo ones we saw on television. Mush, Mush.' He was cavorting around the hall waving an imaginary whip.

The door to the study began to open. Kate had known it would. She gazed at the door fearfully. A murderer was about to emerge — and they were totally at his mercy! What chance had there been for them to creep out unseen and unheard? None! So much for her frantic night-time plan of getting Josef on to a toboggan and escaping to the village! She had known, in her heart, that it was a hopeless idea.

Fatalistically, she waited. What kind of a mood would he be in today? Which Max Heinemann would emerge? The angry, frightened man of last night or the appreciative patient of yesterday afternoon and evening?

Josef stopped and stared, mouth agape.

Kate remembered then, that up until now, he had had no knowledge of anyone else in the house. No wonder he was startled!

As the tall, dark, figure emerged, the surprised child instinctively drew near to his mother. Kate, gazing warily at the sombre-faced fugitive, with a four day growth of beard, caught hold of Josef's hand, protectively drawing him slightly behind her.

Sam, totally unconscious of the atmosphere of suspicion in the room, frisked up to Max, vociferously claiming his attention. He had to be taken notice of before any of them could hear anything else.

'Down, boy,' Max commanded and Sam subsided, recognising the voice of authority and prostrating himself, seemingly glad, Kate thought bitterly, to find a new master in the place.

Max looked at them, taking in the way she was standing in front of her son.

He said heavily, 'I'll help you get the fires going.'

Kate looked at his bandages. She

wondered, without too much compassion, how bad a night he had had. From the look of him, a pretty sleepless one!

'How are you?' she asked stiffly, then without waiting for an answer, added, 'I hope you slept well.'

It was nothing more than appeasement, she was so filled with resentment of his upsetting the first little world that she and Josef had enjoyed in peace that she couldn't have cared less about his night! It was uncharacteristic, but true! So much the better if he had tossed and turned from the pain of his wounds all night, she thought resentfully. He deserved to share her own night fears and wakefulness.

'I'm OK, thanks,' he said. 'This is Josef, is it?' He made an attempt to smile at the child. 'I expect you're hungry for your breakfast.'

Kate, still holding Josef's hand possessively, went towards the kitchen. She could not turn Max Heinemann from the house, but the last thing she was going to do was have him make friends with Josef as he had Sam. It made her blood run cold to think of Josef's innocence in such close contact with a murderer.

'I'm going to get the gas oven going. If you really think you can manage it, I'd like the fire in the living-room started.'

She did not look around again but saw, out of the corner of her eyes, his obedient shuffling walk to the living-room door. Thank goodness he seemed in a conciliatory mood today.

Not that that gave her any comfort. Why should he be anything else? He knew not only that she could provide what he needed, but also that she was powerless to give him up.

She settled Josef at the table and got busy, briskly getting out bacon, eggs and bread. Sustenance was needed to warm them — and the more ordinary an atmosphere she could create, the better for all of them.

Josef was asking in an urgent whisper, 'Who's that man, Mummy? Where did he come from? Is he a friend of ours?'

Kate put three plates to warm and began spreading rashers on to the grill. She considered her answer. Josef must not be over-frightened — on the other hand he must not be allowed to believe Max a sort of uncle with whom he could safely become intimate.

'No, darling, he's not a friend exactly. He's a stranger, but — well, he was hurt — you could see the bandages, couldn't you? So I let him stay here for a while — just while the weather is bad and he starts to get better.'

There was a sound at the door. Kate jumped. She was angry with herself for showing how nervous she was.

'I'm sorry, I didn't mean to scare you,' Max said.

Kate gave him a scorching look, saying evenly, but with a wealth of meaning 'Whether you meant to or not, you certainly succeeded.'

He gave her a hard stare, but did not skirt the issue. 'I suppose you're talking about last night.'

'If you're hurt, why aren't you in

hospital?' Josef asked chattily.

Max looked at him properly for the first time, taking in the huge enquiring brown eyes, black, curly hair, peach-bloom skin and rounded cheeks. He seemed to like what he saw, perhaps the child's easy acceptance appealed to him as much as Sam's undemanding trust had done. This time, when he smiled it was more open.

'I'm not badly hurt. And your mother has patched me up so well that I'm going to get better pretty quickly.'

'Patched you up! Did she use the cartoon sticking plasters? I like them best. How did you get hurt?'

Max seemed to be considering his reply. He finally came out with, 'I was trying to get somewhere really fast and I was silly enough to get entangled with some barbed wire along the top of a stone wall.'

'Ouch!' Josef said screwing up his face in sympathy.

'The trouble was that I was on my own and the more I tried to get free the worse it got. I was stuck there quite a long time — and the snow was falling.'

His face was haunted at the memory. Kate, thinking of the lone, cold, frantically struggling figure he must have been, hardened her heart by recalling what he was and reminding herself that he didn't deserve her compassion.

Josef, of course, had no such reservations.

'Ooh, poor you!' The ghoulishness of the curious child made him enquire interestedly, 'Was there blood all over the snow?'

'Josef, that isn't very nice.' Kate's tone was warning and he hurriedly composed his face into the sympathetic mould again.

'How did you get away? Did someone come along and help you?'

Max's eyes were distant — focused on the memory of pain and anxiety.

'No, there was no-one to help me,' he said slowly. 'I thought I would freeze to death if I stayed there caught by the neck. So I dragged myself clear — it made my leg a lot worse, but at least I was out — and Tamary — your village wasn't far away.'

Kate was once again aware of pity for that desperate man who had been more afraid of being found and recaptured than of causing himself worse injuries. Again she forced herself to banish any softening of her feelings towards him. That was exactly what had got her into this impossible situation!

Silently she put the food on the table. Josef, who was hugely enjoying having someone else to talk to, said positively, 'That's your plate because I don't like tomatoes and neither does Mummy.'

'Thanks. Luckily I do.' Max hesitated only momentarily before he picked up his knife and fork.

They ate without talking. Even Josef was quiet for the moment, being too occupied with his scrambled eggs to have time for conversation!

Kate's brain was busy making a plan, reforming the scheme for their getaway that she had concocted in the darkness of her wakeful night. Perhaps there was a chance she could still take Josef and escape.

After a while, she said, 'I'm going out to the barn for a minute, Josef, to see to the animals. You can come with me.'

For once he was more interested in the stranger than in Delilah and company. He announced loftily that it would be bad manners to leave 'the man' alone, so he would stay indoors and talk to Mr — Mr —

Lost for a name, he looked enquiringly at the stranger.

'You can call me Max. And I'll be delighted to have your company, Josef.'

Oh, but he could be charming when he wanted to be! Kate was furiously irritated at the way he was already ingratiating himself with the child.

'No,' she said sharply. 'You're not staying indoors, you'll come with me to the barn. Go and get your outdoor things, they're on the table in the hall.'

Josef's bright expression faded. He

looked mutinous for a moment but one look at his mother's face was enough to convince him she meant what she said. He blew out his cheeks and gave Max a comical look that plainly said, 'women', before he slid obediently from his chair and left the kitchen.

The smile Max had bestowed on the child, also faded.

'I understand, I suppose! You're not going to let him be alone with the big, bad wolf. Would it be any good to make you a promise that he'd be safe with me? If you remember, I've already promised not to harm you or yours — although that was before I found out you'd been lying to me. Nevertheless, it still stands.'

Kate laughed — a hard laugh without much mirth to it.

'Why on earth should I believe anything — anything at all, that you say? You told me yourself that you're a convicted murderer.'

'Yes, so I did.' He pulled himself to his feet and limped to the door. 'I'll be in the living-room — unless you want me to do anything for you.'

Kate shook her head. 'Just keep the fire going — please.'

'That should be well within my capabilities.' He gave her one scorching look and was gone.

She turned off the gas oven and was getting into her parka and boots when Josef returned, carrying his outdoor things.

'You said you'd like to have a ride on a sledge, didn't you, darling? Well, I've just remembered that there's one hanging on the wall of the barn. When you've helped me with Delilah and Jezebel, I'll pull you along on it — won't that be fun.'

Josef's eyes opened wide. 'Great! But why are you whispering, Mummy?'

Clearly it had not occurred to Max Heinemann that she could possibly get to the village, a mile away, but, with the help of the sledge, she probably could. And even if he came after them, his bad leg would slow him down.

Then, after the police came and

locked him away, she could come back here and take care of everything.

She fed and watered the animals in a mood of growing excitement. No snow had fallen since the day before, and it was no more than knee-deep for her. The toboggan, lifted down and brushed off, was sturdy and had a strong rope attachment.

With the barn door closed behind her, she secured a giggling Josef and began to pull. It slid easily down the path and her optimism grew. It was almost all downhill to Tamary. She knew the road and would try to keep to it, going cross country was too fraught with the perils of falling into ditches. The only difficult bit she would have to traverse would be the humpback piece of road near to the Clapper Bridge.

It took only five minutes of gamely forcing her own legs through the snow, whilst pulling Josef behind her, to realise that the journey was not going to be nearly as trouble-free as she had imagined. Light though he was, the sledge soon began to feel like a ton weight. The road ahead assumed the proportions of a pilgrim's progress — and she was only a hundred yards away from the gate when the sledge tipped and shot Josef off the side.

Panting, she dashed to pick him up, and sit him back on the sledge, afraid he might have hit his head on whatever had caused the fall.

'Oh, darling, I'm so sorry. Are you all right?'

Josef was trying not to cry. The cold snow was filling his mouth, eyes and ears and it was not the friendly stuff he remembered from yesterday. This was icier and altogether harder.

'Let's go home, Mummy. It isn't like on the television. I don't like it.'

She saw, with remorse, that he had hit his head. Like all children, he grew puffy bumps quickly after a blow and there was already an egg-shape one forming above his right eyebrow.

Kate was racked with indecision.

Should she try to soldier on or was it a lost cause before they'd hardly started? Was she, she wondered now, even physically capable of getting them safely to the village? True, it was early in the day, but how dreadful it would be if she stranded them both out here in the pitiless, emptiness of the white moor? It would be taking them out of a potential danger into a real one — the man in the house was more of an unknown quantity than the ferocity of the moor in the depths of winter.

The decision was taken from her hands!

A furious shout came from the house. He had realised that they were gone too long and was coming after them. She saw him emerge from the gate, look both ways and start towards them, limping, but making better headway through the snow than she had with her burden.

Useless to try and escape now! He would catch them before they had covered any distance at all. He reached the sledge first and leaned down to pick up Josef.

'You stupid, little idiot, what possessed you to do such a crazy thing?'

He was talking to her, not the boy, but Kate was conscious only of an appalling revulsion of feeling, as she saw him lift and hold the small figure. To make it worse, Josef put his arms around Max's neck, seemingly thankful to be rescued into big, strong arms. For Kate, it was as though a stream of hatred spread through her mind and body like black ink through her veins. She was possessed by all the devils of hell!

All she could think of was that Josef, her precious son — was being held by hands which had killed, hands which had taken the life of another human being!

'Let him go, don't touch him.' She screamed out and rushed at Max like a virago, beating at him with flailing arms until he released the child and she was able to grab him.

Not unnaturally, Josef began to cry in earnest now. He had never seen his mother with a contorted face, shrieking and punching. Neither had he any memories of being fought over, like a hapless parcel.

Max seemed almost as shocked as the child.

'All right, all right. Good grief, Kate, don't look like that. I wasn't going to hurt him, I was just picking him up.'

Kate was near to hysterical, though, beyond rational thought or conversation. Clutching Josef to her, she stumbled back the way they had come, her face buried in Josef's cold cheek, murmuring soothing words to the sobbing child.

All the way to the house, she ignored the man as though he were not there, conscious only of the need to put one foot in front of the other. Max limped behind her, dragging the sledge, with a strange and thoughtful look on his face, his eyes on the woman and child ahead of him.

When they got to the door, he abandoned the sledge on the path and leaned forward to open it for her. Before she went through, he detained her with a hand on her shoulder.

'Kate, I must speak to you.'

She looked pointedly at the hand, her face as icy as the thin stalactite drips from the eaves of the barn. She said nothing, and after a second he dropped the hand and let her through.

Inside, she put Josef down and began taking off his things. Sam came and barked his displeasure at being left alone. Josef's sobs had turned to gulping hiccups and when he was put beside Benjy in front of the fire, they stopped altogether and he produced a watery smile as the kitten rolled on to it's back waving it's paw in the air.

'It's all right, Mummy. I'm better now.'

'Good. Shall I get you a hot chocolate drink?'

He nodded. She was driven by a need to try and explain the scene outside but judged it better to give him time to get over the shock. Softly, she went from the room, content to let the pets return him to normality.

In the kitchen there was a faint humming sound which Kate, for the moment, did not recognise, until Max Heinemann loomed behind her.

He had taken off Jim's jacket which he had had on, and was wearing blue jeans which were much too big and drawn in with a belt, a check shirt and a thick, Aran sweater, presumably also belonging to Jim.

'The power is back on. Can't you hear it? That's the refrigerator,' he said.

'Oh, good.' She was momentarily too relieved at this news, to hold on to the atmosphere of constraint between them.

'Yes, you're right, I half noticed, when I came in, that the house wasn't as cold.'

'I'm surprised to hear it. I thought you were in too much of a state to notice anything much.'

Without comment she put on a saucepan of milk to heat.

'Would you like a hot drink?' She deliberately avoided looking at him, although she knew that he was trying to make eye contact.

'Thanks. Coffee would be nice. Kate, I have to talk to you.'

'Isn't that what we're doing now?'

'You know what I mean. Really talk.'

'I can hardly prevent you from saying anything you wish to say.'

He gave a twisted smile. 'Except that you're freezing me out. However, I'm going to tell you anyway. Last night — ' He stopped and looked at her. This time Kate met his eyes.

'What about last night?'

'I can't let you go on believing me — what I said I was last night. I thought I could — it maddened me that you'd lied — but when I saw how you reacted to my holding your little boy — outside, in the snow, I just couldn't bear it.'

Kate was utterly still. Somewhere, somehow, the sun was daring to peep out again. If, after all, her instincts had been right, the whole world would look brighter. Ever since he had told her he was a convicted murderer there had been a leaden weight inside her. A disbelief she had had to overcome, a horror of seeing him as a cunning, uncaring killer. Now, if what he was telling her was true, she could begin to see him as a person again. And that, she realised, was what she wanted. Very much!

'Go on.'

He sighed. 'It's difficult. Every prisoner says they're innocent. Why should you believe me, when I say that I was wrongly convicted. But I was, Kate. I swear that I didn't do it. The evidence was circumstantial. I was the obvious suspect. Because Clare — my wife, had left me — gone off with my partner — and taken a large chunk of the profits from the business with her — I was eaten up with malice.'

'If what you say is true, I suppose anyone would be.'

The milk had boiled and Kate poured it into a mug to take into Josef. As she went out of the kitchen she said, 'Put the kettle on, will you? I'll be back in a minute — and we'll talk.'

This time, when his eyes sought hers, she did not avoid them.

She was half-way across the hall when suddenly, shockingly, the front door bell rang!

6

For one catastrophic moment it was as though the whole world had over-reacted to the ringing of the bell.

From the kitchen there was the sound of a chair falling over. Max had jumped up and, in his haste, sent it flying. Now he appeared at the door, almost behind her.

From the living-room Josef and Sam erupted in noisy collaboration, Sam doing his fierce guard dog act and Josef excitedly, and unnecessarily, telling her, 'Mummy, there's someone at the door. We've got another visitor. Mummy, open it. Perhaps it's an Eskimo — or a snowman.'

He giggled, pleased at his own fantasy, but the words, 'another visitor,' had registered on Kate's brain.

Whoever it was, Josef, in his confiding way, would be bound to tell them all about Max. The question was did she want that? Would she have done so first? Or was she going to keep quiet and harbour him?

She was conscious that an agonisingly difficult decision lay ahead of her. To tell or not to tell? It made no difference who was standing outside, that was her choice, to tell or not to tell.

Max had eyes only for her. He stood tall, wild-eyed and vulnerable, staring straight at her, his face a study in urgent desperation. She tried to marshal her thoughts. It all came down to whether she believed him or not.

Yet, surely, if he were as dangerous as she had once thought, he would not be looking at her with such naked entreaty, he would have snatched up some weapon and be prepared to use violence. Perhaps on her, perhaps, God forbid, on Josef, perhaps on the unknown caller.

Could it be the police, still searching for their escaped prisoner?

Max obviously thought so. Not

moving he said, in an urgent whisper, from the kitchen doorway, 'Kate, it was true. Everything I said. I swear to you it's the truth. I had to break out — I desperately need my freedom to prove my innocence. If you give me up now, I'll never be able to. You'd be condemning me to a lifetime of incarceration. Please, don't do it, Kate!'

He was speaking fast, pleading his case, counsel for his own defence.

Kate tore her gaze away and drew a deep breath, forcing herself to deal with the pandemonium boy and dog were creating.

'Quiet, Sam, quiet! Josef go back into the living-room. At once! Did you know that the electricity is back on. You can turn on TV now.'

By telling him that she was hoping to distract him, throw him a sop. For once Josef was not interested in television. He found the idea of yet another unexpected person in his orbit much more interesting! Deaf to his entreaties, she silenced his protests, insisted on his going back to the living-room and tried to ignore the looming presence at the entrance to the kitchen and the final whispered, 'Kate — please.'

Just before she pulled back the bolt, she remembered Sirius. How strange that she had forgotten him and the threat he posed! She marvelled that the fear which had filled her for so long had been driven underground by recent events. One nightmare replacing another!

Thankfully the figure on the doorstep was not her ex-husband and neither was it a policeman. Wearing black clothes, goggles, a woolly hat and skies, he looked like something out of the Winter Olympics! Nothing else registered as Kate waited for him to state his business.

His smile was wide, as his hand went up to lift his goggled on to his forehead.

'Mrs Lennox?'

'Yes. Who are you? What do you want?'

'I hope I didn't give you a fright. Guy

Matthews, Rector of St Michaels, Tamary.'

Only then did she notice the dog collar, showing at the neck of his black anorak. If she had thought about it at all, she would have believed it a polo neck.

Kate tried to remember. Had Jim Carney introduced her to the Rector? And if so, was this the man?

He was looking at her white face and saying regretfully, 'Yes, I did surprise you. I'm very sorry, but we knew you were up here alone and were worried about you. My wife has sent me up with a few things — ' He indicated the pack on his back. 'May I come in?'

Kate stepped back automatically. Her brain was in a whirl. It was fairly certain that the caller was a genuine Good Samaritan, and the least she could do was ask him in, but where could she take him?

Josef and his busy little tongue were settled in the living-room, and Max hidden in the kitchen with no unseen exit except the back door. Perhaps he would go to the barn — she hoped so.

Trying not to think about the option which was still available to her — and perhaps as a public-spirited citizen she ought to use, she said politely, 'It's very kind of you Reverend Matthews, to come all this way — on skis, too.'

'Just Guy, please. All my parishioners call me Guy.'

Clearly a modern cleric, she thought, even with his grey hair!

He had unstrapped his skis and propped them up against the wall outside. Now he was banging the snow off his boots and clothes before stepping over the threshold.

'Mustn't drip all over your hall floor — or rather, I suppose, the Carney's floor.'

Kate smiled as he took his goggles, hat and gloves and, laid them on the table. He had hauled the pack off his back and was rooting in it.

'Let me see now. What have we here? Firelighters and candles, some basic supplies — butter, tea, dried milk — oh, and my wife has sent up one of her home-made cakes. We weren't sure what your needs might be.'

Kate was genuinely touched. Her supplies were still adequate but she felt intense gratitude nonetheless. As well as overwhelming relief that he was not any of the threatening callers she had dreaded!

'You knew that the power was off then? I suppose it was the same in the village. But it's back on now so we've got warmth and light.'

'Really.' The Rector was surprised. 'That's happened since I left home.'

Kate had made up her mind. Perhaps it had been made up long ago! She was going to trust Max and not give him away. As for her unexpected guest, the welcome she had given him had been far less than he deserved and it was time she showed how appreciative she actually was.

'Please come into the living-room,' she said hospitably. 'There's a good fire — my little boy is there at the moment.' Thinking hard she added hastily 'But it's time for his nap. I was just about to take him upstairs. It's very nice to see someone from the outside world. I'll make some tea — unless you'd like something stronger.'

'No, no, tea will be fine.'

He followed her into the living-room where Josef and Sam milled round him and had to be greeted.

'What a dear little cat.' He picked up Benjy and said to Josef, 'this must be yours, for the Carney's had no cat when I last visited them.'

Josef, whose bright eyes had been taking in every aspect of this interesting new visitor, shook his head vigorously. 'He belongs to Mr Carney. But Benjy was brand new when we came. I gave him his name,' he added proudly.

Kate was on tenterhooks, afraid that Josef's alertness would soon lead to a disclosure that they were not alone in the house.

Gravely the Rector complimented

Josef of his choice of name. 'Joseph and Benjamin. They are good Biblical names. They were brothers you know,' he said, winking at Kate, who did not feel equal to telling him the actual spelling of her son's name — or that his father was a Moslem!

'Yes, that's what Mr Carney said,' Josef agreed importantly. 'He said all his animals had always come out of the Bible — once he even had a donkey called Eli — Eli — '

'Elijah,' the Rector supplied helpfully.

Kate was afraid that, at any moment, Josef would recall those present in the house and ask whether Kate and Max were out of the Bible too!

'I'll go and get that tea. But first, Josef, you must go up for your nap.'

Josef was justifiably embittered at being expected to disappear just as the novelty of an outsider had appeared but Kate was adamant. She took him, still protesting, out to the stairs and saw him up to his bedroom, allowing him Benjy for company.

'I'll come and get you in an hour,' she promised guiltily, before squaring her shoulders and entering into the large kitchen cautiously.

She had more than half expected it to be empty with Max having escaped into the barn but, no, he was there, standing behind the door, flattened against the wall.

When she came in, he let out his breath in a sigh of relief, because no-one was with her.

'It's all right!' she reassured him, and then as she made the tea, said, 'I was frightened, too.'

'On my account?' he said, the tension on his features beginning to soften.

Kate's innate honesty broke through again. It would have been nice to let him believe that and bask in his gratitude but she told the truth.

She shook, her head saying, 'Not entirely. I, too, have been running away for years. It could have been — them.'

Max looked thunderstruck. He said sympathetically, 'Poor Kate. You must tell me about that when he's gone. Is that why you understand?'

Kate shrugged. 'Maybe. Anyway it's the local vicar. A nice, kind man. On a mission of mercy because they knew we, Josef and I, were up here alone. There's nothing for either of us to fear from him.'

They had been speaking in whispers but it was probably unnecessary. Josef had left the TV on when he had been rudely plucked away and Guy Matthews, temporarily abandoned by his hostess, was probably watching the one o'clock news and weather report.

'A nice, kind man is he? I'd forgotten such people existed,' Max said bitterly.

Kate had piled the teapot and cups on to a tray and now she went to the door, carrying it. Max stepped forward to hold open the door.

As she passed through, almost as though he could not help himself, he touched her on the cheek with a gentle hand.

116

She was instantly still, gazing up into his face.

He smiled, a slow, sweet smile. 'How could I possibly say that, after what you've done for me, sweet Kate? I'm afraid that prison makes you hard. Unable to believe that anyone does anything unless there's something in it for them. Forgive me — and thank you, for believing in me. I'll never forget it.'

Kate swallowed hard. There was a lump in her throat — a whirl of excitement at his touch — and a kindly clergyman waiting for her in the living-room. No time even to react, no time even to answer Max. She prepared to go in and make polite conversation!

* * *

When darkness came, at half-past four, it was wonderful to have lights once again. Josef was sulking a little at not being allowed to be present while his mother entertained the visitor, but in the evening, Max offered him a challenge at his favourite draughts and let him win by such a narrow margin that Josef was unaware he had been patronised!

Kate made one of Josef's favourite dinners — chicken pie — and they had it on trays by the fire. Later, watching the man and the boy doing a jigsaw together, Kate was filled with the joy of renewed physical comfort from having the house warm and cosy and the serenity of companionable warmth she felt being there with the two of them.

Ridiculous, she told herself sternly, it was all an illusion, a bubble which would burst — but she still enjoyed it.

Once, Max lifted his head and smiled at her, an intimate, only-for-you look, over Josef's head. Recklessly, she smiled back, acknowledging the beginnings of a relationship between them, wondering where this was going to lead them. Coming downstairs, after putting Josef to bed she wondered again. They were alone at last. How would he be? Remembering the gesture of the hand on her cheek, she was half afraid — not of him, she was sure now that he would do nothing to harm her — but of herself.

The depth of her reaction to his touch, made her apprehensive. She was no fool. She knew well that to get involved with a man in the impossible position he was in, would be nothing but folly.

It was proximity, she told herself. Proximity and the pleasure of adult company at last — but she knew, in her heart that it was more than that!

Max made it easy for her. When she came down he was waiting in the hall with both their jackets over his arm.

'May as well go out to the animals before locking up.'

'I've been coping alone with that for months, now, I don't really need any help,' Kate said.

'I know you can, you're extremely capable and have a lot of spirit, but while I'm here I can at least take some of the hard work off your shoulders.'

Absurdly pleased with the compliment, she still tried not to show her pleasure. Instead she looked pointedly at his bandages.

'It was only yesterday that you were looking half-dead. Maybe you should rest. And I'd better take a look at that gash on your neck — and the leg — before bedtime.

'No need. I already have. They're looking good. Another of your successes Mrs Lennox.'

He led the way along the path to the bar. Was it just over twenty-four hours, Kate thought, aloud, that she had half dragged him back to the house?

'Time passes quickly when you're enjoying yourself,' Max said dryly.

It was still quiet, still cold, in the barn.

Clearly Max was used to horses. He limped around the stable, knowing what had to be done without even being told. he had even brought an apple in his pocket for Delilah who nuzzled into him gratefully when he offered it to her.

Kate, busy with fresh hay, had been thinking about what he had said. 'What are my other successes?' she asked innocently and Max laughed at her.

'One day, with luck, I'll be able to tell you,' he said and Kate's eyes dropped before the unmistakable appreciation of the message in his.

When she turned to shut the barn door, she was suddenly in his arms.

Max said, with no more than a tremor in his voice, 'I didn't mean to do that. But, I would like — very much — with your permission — to kiss you.'

Kate looked up at him. In the glow of the yard light and the reflected white of the snow, he looked like some devil-may-care brigand and his dark growth of beard and black hair.

She knew, with aching longing, that she wanted nothing so much as to remain in his arms, but it was all too soon! There was too much at stake. What did he actually feel for her? Gratitude? The desire he would feel for any woman he had met after three years shut away in prison? If so, it wasn't enough.

She knew, with quiet confidence, and growing belief in him as a man of principle, that he would not lower his head and take her lips without some sign from her that his advances were welcome. Raising both her hands she pushed herself back away from his chest.

'No, Max, please let me go.'

His face became shuttered. 'I'm sorry. I shouldn't have asked.'

How quick he was to believe she was rebuffing him, how over sensitive! Kate hurried to explain, morbidly anxious not to hurt him. With some small degree of shyness, she took his hand and held it as they walked back to the house.

'We hardly know each other. I'd like to tell you about — who I'm running away from. You said I should.'

'So I did.' He smiled again but his eyes still searched her face.

'Was it crass of me to believe you are — were — beginning to feel the same way about me as I do about you?' he asked slowly.

Kate hesitated. He was offering her a perfect opportunity to tell him that she felt nothing for him, had no interest in him as a man! But once again, being Kate, she was unable to prevaricate, unable to lie.

'No, you were right, I've felt it, too.'

Again he reached for her eagerly and again she pushed him gently back.

'Please try to understand. I can't afford — can't bear — to get into another relationship that spells trouble. Not again. It was all too painful.'

They were at the door of the house now but before she went in, Max stopped her with a hand on each of her shoulders.

Topaz eyes looked into blue ones, with an intensity that was frightening.

He said sombrely, 'Neither of us can. In one way I dread exposing myself to the ghastly vulnerability that caring about someone brings. But it may be too late now — I think we're already half-way there.'

Kate shook her head in denial and pulled away. How could they be in a relationship without even one kiss? No, she must avoid these moments alone with him. It was the only way to prevent an attachment that, if they succumbed to it, would, she sensed, sweep them away in a fire so strong it could consume them both. Neither of them were lightweight characters, of that she was sure!

It was going to be hard staying apart from him as long as he remained in the house with them. Well nigh impossible in fact!

Unfortunately, for the foreseeable future, there seemed no way to avoid that situation. So all that remained was for her to stay wary — and keep him at a distance, both emotionally and physically!

7

There was an awkwardness about going into the living-room together. They both felt it. Max threw an extra log on to the fire. The house was comfortably warm now, but the fire, with its stone surround, made a cosy focal point.

Kate reflected on how strange it was that this was the first time they had been alone without having urgent things to do, such as tending to his wounds or icy-cold, domestic chores.

Now it was relaxation time — and neither of them quite knew what to do with it — or each other!

Keep him at a distance, she reminded herself!

Max had sat down on the big, square stool in front of the sofa, the better to keep his injured leg straight. He leaned forward, resting his elbows on his knees and waited, serious faced, for Kate to settle herself on the corner of the couch.

Anxious to avoid any kind of tête-á-tête, she said hopefully. 'Would you like me to turn on the TV — or maybe some music?'

He shook his head. 'I'd rather hear about why you were running away.'

'Oh.'

She gazed into the crackling flames for a moment or two, unsure whether she really wanted to evoke the bad memories of her marriage.

Presently she said, 'Yes, I know I said I wanted to tell you, but right now — '

Patiently, Max waited. Finally, watching her face, he put out a hand and rested it over hers.

'Don't tell me if you don't want to. But I'd like to understand you — what makes you tick!'

Kate tried to smile, 'I'm not a time bomb.'

'Aren't you? Don't be too sure of that. I think that, for me, you are.'

Kate decided that asking him what he meant by that was walking on dangerous ground again. Gently she withdrew her hand, not without regret, and said, 'All right, then, here goes.'

She talked steadily, and without much emotion, for a full half hour, until Max knew the whole story.

Once only, after she'd told him about one of the times Sirius had hit her during her pregnancy, did he interrupt, to say, with suppressed passion, 'I'd like to have him here now — to do what he did to you.'

'What good would that do?' Kate asked tiredly. 'Anyway it was all over long ago. The tragedy, as I see it, is that Josef will never know a father — because, although Sirius has sworn to find and kidnap him, he didn't really want him. All he wanted was to get back at me for escaping from him.'

Suddenly it was all too much to take — the recalled moments of fear and terror, the enormous disappointment of knowing that her beautiful son was despised by not only his father but his grandparents, too.

With every intention of remaining detached, Kate was horrified to feel an irresistible sob welling up inside her. She was powerless to prevent it. The strain of the last few days had taken more of a toll on her nervous system than she had realised, so it seemed.

Embarrassed, she quickly put her hands in front of her face, trying to hide her distress from Max but he forestalled her. She meant to get up and rush out of the room, but he was instantly beside her on the sofa and had wrapped his arms around her.

'Let it out, darling. You've had one heck of a raw deal and been coping on your own for far too long.'

In spite of the slipped-out endearment, she was sure he had no ulterior motive, no thought of anything in his mind save the need to comfort her. He was behaving like a good father. Something she badly needed — had needed for a long while! And for the first time since she had been orphaned as a girl she, in turn, felt able to behave like a child — a child who was in need of being protected and loved.

Max held her tightly, in a strong grip, until the first storm of crying had subsided into occasional sobs. It went on for quite a while! Sometimes Kate would murmur something made unintelligible by the gusts of weeping. Occasionally, Max whispered inanities into the hair that was tickling his chin, none of which Kate heard except as reassuring sound.

Finally, when her composure was virtually restored and she began to apologise, he silenced her with a stern finger on her lip.

'If you dare to say you're sorry, for breaking down in front of me, I shall be very angry.'

Through the remains of her tears, with her cheeks still streaked, Kate could not help laughing. 'You sound exactly like a cross grandfather — or schoolteacher.'

He smiled back. 'That's better. Do you want me to let you go?'

Kate looked at the deep, topaz eyes so close to hers. Of course she didn't want him to let her go. Not with her heart! Not ever! So much for her decision to keep him at a distance!

'Yes, please,' she said untruthfully, and felt bereft when he obeyed and took away the comforting shoulder her head had leaned against. He returned to his place in front of the fire.

There was a short silence. Kate, afraid of what either of them might do or say to fill it, asked, 'Would you turn on the news please? It would be a good idea if we knew what weather to expect tomorrow.'

Max leaned forward and switched on the television. With startling unexpectedness they were confronted with a picture of him!

Kate gasped and would have spoken but Max, his face a mask of intentness, said sharply, 'Listen. I need to know what they say.'

'The prisoner who escaped from Princetown jail, five days ago, has not been traced and is believed to be out of the area,' the announcer informed them crisply.

Max grinned and waved a triumphant fist in the air.

'Police are confident that he had an accomplice waiting with a vehicle. The severity of the weather means that, without help, he would, by now, either have died from exposure or have been forced to give himself up.'

Another photograph was thrown up on the screen, this time showing the gaunt greyness of Dartmoor, with the prison surrounded by snow.

The newscaster had not finished with the story yet.

She went on, 'However, the authorities wish to warn the general public that the man is extremely dangerous and should not be approached in any way.' Again the picture changed and a 'mug shot' of a younger and villainous-looking Max appeared on the screen, a full face and a profile side by side.

He looked quite unlike the lean-faced

man with a growing beard sitting cosily with Kate beside the fire. Glaring and hard-eyed, he looked, in fact, exactly like someone about whom a casual observer might say, 'Well you can see he'd murder his own mother can't you?'

Max stared at the picture resentfully. 'It's a rotten likeness! I look like Jack the Ripper. They took that when I arrived. I felt as though I was being buried alive. They strip all your dignity — you even lose respect for yourself. Wasn't it a good thing we didn't have the early evening news on? I would have hated Josef to have seen that.'

Kate did not answer. She could not! All the earlier fears had returned. The moment that picture had flashed into her living-room and the announcer, later, had said 'extremely dangerous' she had been flooded with renewed anxiety. She wondered, all over again, what on earth she was doing, what crazy chance she was taking, by harbouring a convicted criminal.

Max looked round. He saw her face,

and knew instantly what she was thinking. He said sharply, 'Kate,' but she eluded his outstretched hand, jumped to her feet and made for the door.

'I'm going to bed,' she said abruptly, her whole body rigid with tension.

He had been taken by surprise and was a little off-balance but nonetheless he was incredibly quick, in spite of his limp, in catching up with her. By then she had reached the bottom step of the staircase.

When his hand grasped her shoulder, Kate shook it furiously off.

'Don't touch me,' she cried, and then, from the depths of misery and mistrust that she hated renewed, she snapped, 'That's all you've done this evening — grabbed at me. Let me alone.' The hand dropped to his side as though he had been scalded.

He stepped back, saying broodingly, 'I suppose I know what brought this on. But it surely didn't change anything. If you can believe — '

133

Kate burst out, 'What I believe or don't believe is immaterial now, isn't it? I've done exactly what the police recommended people not to do — hidden you. I must be a gullible idiot.'

Max's expression hardened. Lips tightly compressed he made no attempt to persuade her otherwise or protest his innocent. He said nothing but when, after waiting a moment, Kate turned and hurried up the stairs, his eyes followed her with painful intensity.

Regardless of the fact that it hurt his neck to raise it to the angle necessary to watch her progress, his gaze did not waver. He watched the passage of the slight, hurrying figure all the way across the landing until she disappeared from view. If he had hoped for any further acknowledgement of his waiting presence he was disappointed! Kate looked neither to right nor to left until she was out of his sight.

★   ★   ★

By the next morning the thaw had begun in earnest. Kate woke to the sound of dripping water, thankful, at least, that it was outside. She did not relish having to cope with any flooding from frozen pipes and was thankful that the Carney's plumbing and heating was modern and efficient!

Dawn, and a pale sun emerging at last, had brought a calmer mood. She was amazed at her own waverings. Having decided that she believed in Max, why should a news item — which did no more than reiterate the facts she knew already — have caused her such traumatic uncertainty! It was, she decided, ridiculous. She was making a mockery of her own instincts. Her instincts told her to believe in him. He was no longer just a mysterious stranger, he was Max, a man with gentle eyes and hands, who had scrupulously avoided forcing himself on her, who had wanted to but held back, a man, moreover, who liked children and animals.

Perhaps it was an irrational decision, certainly it was a risky one, but all her being sensed that he could be trusted. And trust him she would!

Today she would tell him so — before apologising for her unjust behaviour last night.

When she had broken down, what a tower of strength he had been for her comfort! And what had she done to repay him? Turned on him like a virago! She was filled with regret and could hardly get dressed quickly enough, in her impatience to see him, explain and put things right.

Josef was still cuddled down in bed, and she did not disturb him. By the time he woke properly she would have a hot breakfast ready for them all.

The hall was unusually quiet and empty. Neither Sam nor Max were anywhere to be seen, but Kate was untroubled by their absence. He had probably gone out to the barn, taking the dog with him, and would be back presently. Then she would have her opportunity to set the record straight!

She got busy in the kitchen and was beating eggs in a bowl when the telephone rang.

The unexpected shrilling was such a shock that Kate dropped the bowl. It clattered on to the floor and she stood there, too surprised even to notice the yellow mixture oozing around her feet.

By the third or fourth ring, she had got over her shock and run into the hall to lift the receiver. She was busy rationalising. There was no need to be afraid of anything. All it meant was that the lines had been repaired and someone — the rector perhaps — was ringing to let her know and to check on her well-being.

'Hello.' She had long ago stopped giving her name, deeming it wiser, in case Sirius was on her trail, to wait and let the caller identify themselves first.

'Hello, is that Mrs Lennox — the little boy's mother — staying at the Carney place?'

The caller was obviously not young

and obviously from Devon.

Out of a tremendous relief that it was not the police and not the ones she had feared Kate said, 'Yes. Can I help you.'

A rich laugh echoed on her ears. 'It's more a case of me hoping to help you. You came into my shop with Jim Carney. D'you remember me, now?'

'Oh, before they went away.' The village store, Kate remembered, had old-fashioned counters, a small Post-Office and a jolly, large lady along the same lines as Mrs Carney herself.

'Well, dear, Jimmy, my son, has got chains on the van and he's doing a delivery today. I expect he'll get as far as you, now the snow's clearing. So if there's anything we can send out?'

Kate began to say, 'It's very — ' when she was suddenly held painfully tightly from behind. A vice-like grip went round her waist and a gloved hand covered her mouth.

Mutely she gazed up at her attacker, unable to speak a word, unable to believe he was doing this to her.

Max muttered fiercely, 'Answer them. Make it good! I'm going to take my hand away. One word — just one wrong word.'

Kate's eyes stared into his wild and angry ones, unable even to move her head, because it was jammed back against his shoulder. Slowly, so slowly, he eased the hand away from her mouth.

The voice on the other end was saying, 'I think there's something wrong with the line, dear, did you say something?'

Trying to think clearly Kate gasped out, 'It — it was very nice of you to call. But the Carney's were very far-sighted. I have plenty of dried foods — and I'm still using up all the freezer stuff because of the power cut.'

'So you're OK.'

'Yes, thank you. But I'll come down to the village and stock up as soon as the roads clear a bit. I can.'

'All right then, dearie. My number's

139

in the book if you need anything. Cheerio, then.'

'Yes, goodbye,' Kate said softly.

The phone went dead again and the receiver dropped from her nerveless hand.

The black tide of fury in the eyes so close to her own had faded back to the clear topaz. Max did not let her go, but there was a subtle difference in the way he was holding her.

He groaned in deep contrition and dropped his head on to her shoulder. Kate, in spite of her fright and anger, felt a stirring of feeling at his closeness.

'Oh, Kate. I'm sorry, I'm so damned sorry. I've made a mess of it again! Kate, I can't begin to tell you what I thought. Coming into this room and finding you on the phone. After last night I thought — I thought you were trying to give me up.'

Kate's overwrought nerves were threatening once again to bring on a bout of tears. It seemed particularly hard — particularly ironic — that he should have failed to trust her after her eager anticipation of seeing him this morning and telling him face to face that she believed in him. Suddenly, she was filled with overflowing resentment.

Always — always — she had determined not to feel sorry for herself but now waves of self-pity were washing over her. And she, a girl who never swore, began to shriek at him and hit out hysterically.

'You pig, you — you — How could you believe that? How could you? I didn't give you any — Let me go. I hate you.'

The hand that had been on her mouth was on her neck, the one on her waist, instead of violently restraining her was turning her towards him.

'Darling, I'm sorry, I'm so sorry.'

He was caressing her, as though he could not help himself, trying to show, by touch, the depths of his repentance.

As a man in slow motion, following a time ordained path, he had lowered his lips to meet hers — and Kate, forgetting all thoughts of keeping her guard up, responded to the intimacy of his touch like someone coming home at last.

The kiss was sweet, the embrace compulsive and neither of them were aware of anything other than each other.

Only when both had to pull away in order to breathe, did their mouths part company. Then Max said brokenly, 'Kate, Kate, sweet Kate, I think I've been wanting to do this since you stood over me in the barn and threatened me with that empty rifle.'

Shakily, still overwhelmed by the depth of the feelings he was inspiring in her, but ever practical, Kate said, 'No you didn't, you felt much too ill.'

He was stroking her cheek, touching her eyebrows, gazing into her face with a sense of wonder, but at this down-to-earth response he laughed.

'You're such a realist. And I love you for it — and other things! Is that how it's always going to be for us — love and laughter?'

Instantly both of them sobered up from the pink cloud they were temporarily sharing.

'Always?' Kate asked. 'The way things are with us we may not have an always.'

'I know.' Max's face held no laughter now. He said wretchedly, 'I'm a villain to have let it happen. You don't need someone like me. You've had enough troubles in your life. But it's too tempting — after what Clare did — my ex-wife — and what happened to me, I never dared to think that anyone would love, trust or want me again. Let alone a lovely girl like you. I just don't deserve you, sweet Kate.'

He had been so badly hurt! Kate's heart twisted with pity — and something like hatred for the woman who had done it to him.

She was filled with a desire to show him just how much she wanted him. Raising her face she brought it once again to his and waited expectantly and was dazed with surprise when he sprang away from her.

'Listen,' he whispered urgently. 'Josef! He's coming across the landing.'

Yes, he was right, there was a slight movement upstairs and Kate heard the yawn she recognised as the sound a sleepy little boy made soon after waking.

When Josef's foot touched the top stair, his mother was nowhere in sight but he could hear her bustling about in the kitchen. She was mopping up a pool of spilled egg! Max was at the front door calling to Sam. He turned and grinned at Josef.

'I'm as hungry as a hunter. How about you?'

'Me, too.' Josef picked up the kitten which had strolled up and was rubbing against his legs. He followed Max into the kitchen and was soon munching his way happily through two bacon sandwiches. To Josef everything appeared normal. He was totally unaware of the consciousness of each other the adults were experiencing

— or the long looks they exchanged over his head.

For them nothing was normal. Nothing, in fact, would ever be the same again!

8

It took another week for the snow to go. The snow-plough had managed to clear the roads once the weather had abated a little but after it had been through, the hedges and ditches were packed with black-edged compressed drifts which continued to freeze at night. And with the stone walls beneath and behind them, driving was like going through a white corridor in many places.

For Kate, it was one of the happiest weeks of her life! She was in a cosy, exciting, brand-new world — a world inhabited only by man, woman and child! Each day, she and Max discovered new facets of each other, peeling away layers of prejudice, disillusionment, and guardedness, and taking joy in their discoveries.

It was wonderful. All of it! Watching Josef follow Max about, knowing he had a male figure who, to her delighted wonder, seemed to be made in the shape of the role model she had always wanted for him.

It was bliss to sit in the firelight hand in hand with Max in the evenings, discovering for the first time, what togetherness, support and companionship meant.

She never wanted it to end, she could have gone on living so for ever. Yet all the time there was a shadow just behind them. The knowledge, pushed for the moment to the back of their minds, that both of them were fugitives on the run. Like cave dwellers, they lurked in their hideaway and played, with the world and its dangers waiting for them outside the boundaries!

One day Nemesis had to catch up with them, she knew that, even while she rejoiced in the present — and yearned for it to continue. If only they could all be left alone to live in peace.

The wounds on Max's neck and leg healed rapidly.

'Thanks to you,' he said warmly, displaying dressing-free scars for her inspection.

He had taken much of the work of the house and animals away from her, in spite of her protests. Josef, endlessly prattling, was now one of two shadows glued to Max's heels — the other being Sam — and it gave Kate infinite pleasure to see the patience with which the man answered her child's questions.

Both her love and her admiration for him grew daily. They shared a common, often unspoken bond, a rapport she would not have believed possible between two comparative strangers.

Then one day a card came from California.

Hearing the letter-box flap go, Kate went out and picked it up from the mat, making a mental note that she must remind Max to take care when going in and out of the barn. He and his disciples were out there now, returning Delilah to her stall after the exercise he gave her daily, but it would certainly not do to become careless now that the postman — and maybe others — was coming to the house.

She read the friendly message with mixed feelings. It was nice to be remembered, they were good people — but the card was an unwelcome reminder that the world was still out there — and could not be lost for love!

There were sounds of laughing, and a noisy arrival, as man and boy came through the kitchen door, Josef erupting through it like a small tornado, before throwing himself on to a chair.

Max's eyes, as always after a parting, no matter how short, meeting hers in the searching, intimate look which telegraphed his wish not to be away from her for too long. She met it fully, only a slight blush revealing how shy she sometimes still was with him!

'Look, Josef,' she said, holding the card out to him. 'Mr and Mrs Carney have been all over the place and they've sent us a postcard.'

Josef giggled. 'The other Mr Carney's

nearly all gone now — there are just his knees left.'

Kate looked blank for a moment and Max said easily, 'The snowman, dar — Kate.'

'Oh.' Her expression warned him to be more circumspect. Calling her darling in front of Josef was just not on — whether or not the child would recognise any significance in such lover-like terms, she did not want to upset his equilibrium.

Max put on a wry, apologetic expression, and Kate, choosing her words carefully, said, 'The postman may be coming everyday now. His van is red.'

Josef, through a mouthful of cereal, started to sing 'Postman Pat,' but Max nodded.

'I'll watch out for him,' he said gravely and Kate knew he understood what she had been getting at.

Later in the day though, soon after lunch, with a watery sun trying to promise warmer days, something happened which made her reproach herself for becoming too relaxed.

Max had gone out through the back door to cut and bring in their supply of logs for the fire. Josef, who had woken early, was up in his room with Benjy and some picture-books. Kate, who had noticed black marks around the front door, had put on jacket and gloves and gone out to the porch with a cloth and some cleaner. She was quite determined that the Carneys should find their home in good condition when they returned.

Though the air was still icy, it was pleasant with the unaccustomed bright-ness from the sun and she rubbed away with a will, her new-found euphoria finding expression in singing a few snatches of song — which was probably why she did not hear anyone approach!

They were on the steps, close behind her before she knew.

A middle-aged couple, the woman wrapped in a fur coat and the man wearing a cap and heavy sheepskin jacket. Solid, bespectacled individuals.

With a red BMW parked at the end of the drive behind them.

Aghast, Kate stared at them, her duster in one hand and the bottle of cleaner in the other. She wondered whether she could lean against the doorbell. If she did would it be warning enough for Max to stay away? Or would he think she was summoning him and come rushing in?

The man made a production out of pulling off a driving glove and holding out his hand.

Flustered, Kate stuck the duster into her pocket and took it. He shook hers firmly, and indicated his wife.

'Elspeth and George Fawley. Driven over from Tavistock. We're friends of the Carneys. Play Bridge with them. We heard all about you.'

The woman had drawn level now and shaken Kate's hand as well.

'George thought it was about time we had a little fresh air. We've all had to hibernate lately or we would have come over before.'

She drew the edges of the fur coat more tightly around her, saying, with a shiver, 'Mind you, this is a bit too much fresh air out here.'

Kate stood stock-still in an agony of apprehension. If she asked them in — which of course they expected her to do — they might see Max. If she didn't they would certainly think it strange and it could stir up gossip.

'How — how nice of you to call,' she said and discovered that she really had no say in choosing to allow them into her house. Elspeth had already stepped by her, and in through the door, removing her scarf as she went.

George was chivalrously holding his arm out, indicating that Kate should precede him into the house.

Clearly they both knew their way around inside. Elspeth had opened the living-room door and was walking up to the fireplace, putting out her hands to get the warmth.

'Oh, dear, if I'd known just how bitter it still was, I'd have stayed home,

George.' She turned to Kate. 'Do you mind if I have a drop of Jim's whisky, I need something to take off the chill — and he wouldn't mind.'

Kate went to the table where the Carneys kept their small store of alcohol. Since the night she had given it to Max as an anaesthetic there was even less!

Without speaking she poured a measure and gave it to the woman. George, however, shook his head. Both of them had divested themselves of their coats — though Elspeth kept hers draped over her shoulders — and showed every evidence of making a long stay.

'Well now,' Elspeth began, after a searching look around the room to see if Kate had made any changes, 'Isn't this nice?'

Kate had not missed her sharp-eyed scrutiny of everything, and knew resentfully that these people, the woman anyway, had come to see what she was up to and to ferret out everything about her. They were curious and had whiled away a boring afternoon by coming over to pump the 'house-sitter' at Jim's place. That was obvious!

Well, she'd not learned to cover her back over the last few years without being able to parry amateur inquisitors like this. She prepared to do some stonewalling. The only wonder was that they were friends of the easygoing Carney's! She could not conceive of a more unlikely pair as buddies of her warmhearted hosts. Probably George was exaggerating, she shrewdly surmised, and they were actually no more than cardplaying acquaintances.

They had been talking no more than five minutes, with Kate managing to give ambiguous answers to unashamedly personal questions, when the door opened and Max, with a bundle of logs in his arms, walked in.

For a second or two, no-one spoke at all, two of them being dumfounded with surprise, he with startled amazement and something like horror.

Kate was the only one of those present who had known that this could happen. She had already prepared herself for what she would do should Max walk in. Getting quickly to her feet, she spoke in an artificially clear and steady tone, hoping that no-one would hear the tell-tale wobble in her voice.

'Ah, there you are, darling. You must let me introduce my husband, Tom. Tom this is Mr and Mrs Fawley, they're friends of the Carneys.'

There was a pregnant pause. Kate hoped desperately that Max would follow her lead. She was trying frantically to recall what she had told the Carneys. But even then, there was a possibility they had not passed much information on except that she was alone up there and had a child with her.

'We understand you were on your own here — with your little boy,' Elspeth said sharply.

Kate was more than ready for that question and said smoothly, 'Yes, I was when I came, but Tom finished his — project — sooner than we expected. Wasn't it lucky for me that he could join us?'

Max had grasped what she was trying to do. Giving himself time to think, he put the logs down beside the fire, slowly wiped his hands on his jeans and held one out to George Fawley.

'You're the first people, except the Rector, that have come to call. We must thank you for giving us a taste of the neighbourhood.'

Having speedily taken Elspeth's measure, he then bestowed a warm, friendly smile on her.

Flattered, she relaxed and changed her suspicious manner into one of receptiveness.

Kate's stomach was churning, but she was able to appreciate Max's strategy. The woman led the way in this set-up and Max was using his undoubted charm on her. Kate watched and listened as he swung immediately into easy sociability with this rather pushy and provincial couple.

She was enormously proud of him. It seemed strange that they knew each other so well now, yet she had never before seen him in company with others.

Remembering the mug-shot on the television she was thankful that he looked nothing like it. His beard was properly established now, and his longer hair and the collar of his shirt hid the scar at his neck.

A new worry reared its head as he got up to pour Elspeth another drink. How well did they know Jim Carney's wardrobe? She prayed that they had never seen the blue, denim shirt and black sweater that Max was wearing.

After fifteen minutes they were showing signs at last of getting ready to leave, gathering together their things, talking of how quickly the darkness came at this time of the year.

Kate, in an agony of impatience for them to leave would have sped them through the door immediately, but Max gave the impression of being totally unhurried. Even so, they had got to the hall and he was about to open the front door, when another potential danger reared it's ugly head. Josef, rubbing his eyes, appeared at the bottom of the stairs.

Kate's throat constricted in anxiety. Never had she been less enthusiastic at the sight of her son. Poor lamb, it was too bad that he should have awoken just now. One second later and they would have been gone!

Now anything could happen. One of them would ask him archly if he wasn't a lucky boy to have his daddy with him, he would look amazed and ask them what they meant, or he would call Max by his name and all would be lost.

His temporary 'father' showed no outward signs of worry at all. Smiling he went to the stairs and scooped Josef up into his arms, bringing him back to the group, telling him, 'This is Mr and Mrs Fawley, Josef, say hello to them.'

Meanwhile, Elspeth, turning to Kate, said effusively, 'Oh, is that your little boy? My, he certainly is like his father.'

She meant Max, of course. The thought had not entered Kate's head until this moment, but now she saw, with secret pleasure, that there was a superficial resemblance. Mostly because they were both very dark, with wide set eyes.

'Yes, so I'm told,' she said before changing the subject quickly. Feigning a start of surprise, she asked, 'Was that a thunderclap I heard?'

'You did?' Elspeth was immediately diverted. Twice during their conversation she had expressed a wish to be back before dark. Now she turned to her husband and almost pushed him out through the door.

'Nice to have met you all. Come along, George, if there's going to be a storm — and I must say the sky looks awful — I want to be back home before it starts. Goodbye, all.'

George was engaged in bestowing a fifty-pence piece in Josef's hand. 'For a few sweets,' but when he heard the summons, he hastily pulled on his gloves and followed his wife down the drive.

The last sight of them was Elspeth's regal hand waving from the window of the red car.

'Phew!' Kate breathed a sigh of relief, as she shut the door.

Max had put Josef down and was grinning at her.

'Masterly,' he said teasingly, 'making a clap of thunder. And I was interested in the resurrection of brother Tom! Except now I seem to be playing the part — and he's a husband!'

He took her chin between finger and thumb, whispering, for her ears only, 'I certainly wish that I was your husband.'

Josef looked up and Max said, more loudly, 'Can't say I'm sorry they're gone. For all sorts of reasons. Our Elspeth is not, I'm afraid, a lady I'd choose to spend the afternoon trapped in a lift with. One can only feel a certain amount of sympathy for the hapless George, he might as well have a collar and lead!

Josef showed his mother his new largesse. 'Shall we have more visitors tomorrow?' he enquired hopefully, visions of great wealth clearly dancing before his eyes.

'I sincerely hope not,' Kate said, puffing out her cheeks. 'I must have aged ten years today.'

'Thanks again, sweet Kate,' Max said softly. 'Once again, I'm in your debt. You were wonderful.'

Kate, in the aftermath of the fright she had had, was experiencing reaction and wanted nothing so much as to be enfolded into his arms, but that had to wait. With Josef present, all he could give her was a smile. Though even a smile, she discovered, if it held meaning and depth, and if the eyes crinkled at the corners and expressed loving appreciation, could be a sort of caress!

9

It was three days after the visit of the Fawleys and life had settled into a cosy domestic routine. They had even begun taking moor walks, mostly in the morning and well away from the roads. Since no-one else was mad enough to brave the cold it was reasonably safe. The few walkers they did see, thought nothing of a small family party such as they appeared to be and as Kate wished passionately that they were!

She felt she had never known what happiness was until she had watched a laughing Josef being swung around by Max while the dog ecstatically barked at them and she watched, smiling.

'Again, Max. Again,' Josef pleaded, clinging to the long, jeans-clad legs of the grinning man.

Max, smiling down at him, involuntarily winced, and Kate said quickly,

'Mind your bad leg.'

'It's fine.'

To prove how well his wounds had healed, he hauled Josef up to ride on his shoulders.

'Just hold on to my head, son, not my neck.'

Later when they were in the kitchen sipping an evening cup of coffee, with Josef already in bed upstairs, Max said abruptly, 'I have to go, you know.'

A remembered line of verse came into Kate's head, 'Come live with me and be my love.' That was what Max had done and now he was telling her that it was coming to an end.

'Go?' She could not hide the desolation within her, at the thought of losing him.

'You knew I had to some time.'

He reached across the table and clasped both her hands in his. 'It's paradise being here with you, but we can't live like this for ever. We're just fooling ourselves — shutting out the rest of the world — and it could only be a sham until I've proved my innocence. Kate, my love, I have to get to London and set in motion the things I escaped to do.'

Kate's hands turned under his, the better to hold them.

With all her being she wanted to cry out, 'No, no stay here. Don't risk being caught. Stay with me for ever,' but all she said was a quiet, 'I know.'

She swallowed painfully, past the lump in her throat, determined not to break down.

'I knew — of course I knew — it had to come soon. I kept trying not to think about it. We've had a winter idyll — and idylls don't last.'

'Don't talk like that.' Max sounded stern. 'As though everything is over. If all goes right — if I can do what I set out to do — we can be together properly.'

'There's still Sirius,' Kate reminded him miserably.

'Yes, and that's another reason why I hate to leave. Apart from the obvious one, that I love you.' He punctuated this speech by leaning across the table and giving her a butterfly kiss on the lips, no more than a glancing pressure. 'Have you any reason to think he's got any notion where you might be?' he asked anxiously.

'No, none at all,' Kate assured him. 'I hope that he's lost the trail.'

Outside the window where the yard light was illuminating the path, it was a frosty, glistening ice-rink, and they both turned their heads to look at it, laughing at the unconscious aptness of her words.

'You're so right,' Max said wryly, 'that trail is very bold indeed.'

Still holding her hands, he pulled her slightly towards him and gave her a long, loving look.

'You've been magic, Kate. You've brought me back to life — in every way.'

There was something starkly final about the past tense. Kate wanted desperately to hold on, to find a way of preventing him from going, but she couldn't — and wouldn't. For his sake, she had to let him go, without making it any harder for him.

With a ghost of a smile she joked lightly, 'A man's gotta do, what a man's gotta do.'

Max was not deceived. They were too close now and he understood and ached for her pain, as well as his own.

'If only I could be sure that blasted ex-husband of yours wasn't hovering anywhere. You need protection.'

Kate picked up their empty mugs and went to the sink to rinse them.

'I've managed without any protection for quite a long time now. Anyway, he may have given up and gone home.'

Max, still sitting down, put out his arms, grasped he round the waist and pulled her towards him. He pressed his head against her, sighing deeply.

Kate looked lovingly down at the dark head, and ran her fingers through his hair. he looked up and she transferred a hand to the silky softness of his beard.

'Should I shave?' he asked teasingly.

'No, of course not, it's a proper

— and very handsome — beard now. You look like an upmarket pirate. Not a bit like those horrible pictures they showed on television.'

Max got up, still holding her, and for a moment they clung tightly, lost in the wonderment of each other.

'Tomorrow, I think,' he said reluctantly.

'So soon?' Kate was aghast. 'Just a few more days, Max,' she pleaded.

'The day after, then,' he conceded, sublimely unaware of what a momentous decision he had made. Or what a difference it would make to both their lives. 'Until then — we must make the most of what we've got, darling.'

He bent his head and kissed her, this time more roughly, but long and passionately, drinking in her sweetness while he still had time . . .

The next day dawned bright and sunny, though the air was edged with a Siberian chill. Kate had known for days that it would be necessary to make a trip to the local stores soon and decided that

168

she would go this morning while the sun shone.

If Max was really leaving them soon, she wanted to make a special meal, a special occasion of his last evening, and for that she needed fresh milk, fruit, and vegetables.

She told Josef at breakfast and he was loud in his demands to come with her to the village.

'But, Josef, I'm only going to the village for groceries and things. Wouldn't it be more interesting to stay home with Max and Sam than trail round the shops after me?'

For an answer he dug into his trouser pocket, triumphantly removing his precious fifty pence. 'I want to spend this,' he announced importantly.

'All right then,' Kate said. She handed Max the keys to the car. 'Would you warm the car up for us — I'll put on his snowsuit and be on the doorstep in five minutes.'

It felt strange to be driving around the village street, and to find, somewhat surprisingly, that so many of the local people had either heard of her or were anxious to be friendly. She met the Rector's wife who immediately suggested they have coffee together. Kate would have liked to have accepted but was afraid of what Josef might blurt out. Luckily the Fawley's lived in Tavistock so presumably the arrival of her 'husband' had not been communicated to the Tamary community!

She saw a notice offering car hire at the garage and it crossed her mind that she could arrange for a car for Max, when he left, in her name. She would gladly have lent him the one the Carney's had left, had it been hers but it seemed wrong to do so without their permission. Besides, she really needed it.

Enjoying the sunshine and the heady excitement of being out again, Kate's usual vigilance was suspended. Apart from which, her head was too full of her feelings about Max leaving, and the problems associated with that, to be as aware as usual of any suspicious circumstances. A fact for which she was to pay dearly!

She failed to notice a white car come out of a side road and fall in behind her as she approached the village. Talking to Josef and consulting her list, she did not, as she had in the past, look carefully around, and take note of any unusual strangers. So she entirely missed the heavily built man in his forties, who got out of a parked car across the street, and ostensibly paused in a doorway to light a cigarette.

He went into the estate agents while she was in the store, because from there he could watch the store through the agents window.

Later, while she chatted to the Rector's wife on the pavement, he pretended to scrutinise the objects in the antique dealers window.

When Kate went back to her car it took her a while to get Josef strapped on to his booster seat and lift all her purchases into the back. The unknown watcher was much quicker. He slipped into the driver's seat of his white saloon and slid out from the kerb and away from the village ahead of Kate.

He had made his plan and knew what he was going to do. When she got to the end of the village street and took the road for the farm he was already out of sight.

Josef was in cheery mood on the way home. The proud possessor of a small selection of mixed goodies, he was investigating the bag and loudly informing the interested, the sequence in which he would demolish the contents. So he was much put out when his mother stopped so suddenly that his sweet bag was jerked from his hand.

Kate herself was startled, but not yet frightened!

They had been nearly home, just yards from the gate in fact, when the white Saloon had come streaking towards them. On the narrow road she had had no choice other than pull sharply up.

Shaken and rather cross, she held her hand hard down on the horn — he had been going much too fast — then indicated, by putting on the left flasher, that she meant to go into the gate. Annoyed, but not otherwise alerted, she waited impatiently for the other car to retreat. It was only when he made no attempt to do so and instead, got out and came towards her, that fear grew.

The big, thick-set man was moving quickly, making a dash, not to the front seat, where she sat, nor to her car door but to the back door — and Josef.

A sickening sense of having all her nightmares come true washed over Kate as she realised that she had even been slack enough, this once, not to have locked the car doors.

Yet, even in the midst of her sudden panic, she was puzzled. He was not the kind of man she had dreaded — he was nothing like the young, dark, associates of Sirius that she had believed, for years, would come and try to take her son away from her.

Gasping, she wrenched at her own door and opened it in his way — managing to halt the assailant's rush, temporarily. For a moment he was winded but it was no more than a flea trying to stop a tank. Without compunction, he hauled her roughly out, pushed her to the ground and had put his hand on the back door, all in virtually one powerful movement.

Heedless of her bruises, Kate screamed, 'No!' and reached desperately for his leg, hoping to pull him off balance. From inside the car, Josef, seeing his mother knocked down, began to cry in terror.

The man tugged at the door, and, when he had got it open, tried to lift out the frightened child. When he discovered the car seat straps prevented him he cursed furiously and worked at them with his free hand. They were designed to be undone quickly in an emergency, and he had little difficulty with them but by the time Josef was in his grasp, Kate had struggled to her feet and flung herself at him in a frenzy of flailing arms.

Josef, piteously sobbing, was reaching out his hands for her, and Kate caught hold of him, too, determined to cling on, desperately trying to prevent the attacker from getting away.

Again he swore and hit out at her, but he was hampered now by having to hold on to the boy. Kate took a blow to the face and was cut on the forehead by a ring he was wearing. She was conscious of a sharp pain, but somehow kept her grip on her son.

Only when, by sheer strength, the man forced her once more to the ground did she begin screaming despairingly.

'Josef! No! Josef!'

She was in an agony of fright! If he got away with Josef she might never see him again. Even through the blood running down her forehead and into her eyes that was all she could think about.

He had almost reached the Saloon with the terrified little boy held now under one arm, when Max appeared at the gate.

One comprehensive look told him all he needed to know. He had realised something was wrong, of course, when he first heard the horn pressed. Then the screaming had alerted him to its being a crisis of some kind, but until he had come in sight of the cars he had believed it might be strangers — someone who had had an accident perhaps and whom he could help. The scene before him told its own story. Josef was being kidnapped!

Every instinct in Max wanted to go to Kate. Kneeling by the side of the road, she was covered in grass and mud, and fighting to get back to her feet. Max resisted the urge. He knew what had to be done and what she would want him to do more than anything else. Ignore her and save her child!

At least he had the advantage of surprise! The kidnapper had had no idea that a man was in the house and his face, as Max surged toward him, expressed anger and chagrin. Women and children he could deal with, but a man was a different matter!

Max came at him and he instinctively dropped Josef and squared up.

Max was tall and lean. The stranger was much heavier and older as well. Nonetheless, Max still had scars and a weak leg. Not that he thought about that at all! If ever there was murder in a man's heart, it was in Max after seeing Kate in a battered state, crying and distressed. Rightly or wrongly, he was motivated for revenge.

Josef, finding himself on the grass, at the side of the road, crawled away and towards his mother. She had managed to pull herself upright now, brushed the blood out of her eyes with a hand and was ready to meet him and grasp him convulsively to her.

With him hugged to her, she watched in horror as the two men hit out at each other, agonisingly fearful for Max.

The older man clearly knew nothing and cared less about Queensberry

Rules! And when Max sustained a kick which forced a groan from him and sent him reeling back against the bonnet of the white car, Kate was suddenly possessed of a need to find some way of helping him.

With shaking hands and murmurs of reassurance, she bundled the crying but unresistant Josef into the car. She looked wildly around for a weapon and found it on the floor of the car. One of her shopping bags contained several tins of dogfood! Picking it up, and taking a firm grasp, she locked the car door, dropping the keys into her jacket pocket.

Thankfully, Max had ducked the blow that was meant to finish him off and was once more wrestling with the unknown man, from whom grunts of effort seemed to indicate that he was losing stamina. Both were breathing heavily but neither had eyes to spare for anything but each other.

Kate attacked the man without a second thought. She lifted the bag and brought it down with all her strength, hard on the side of the kidnapper's head.

He was not knocked out but he was hurt. A groan of pain escaped him but it was his astonishment at the unexpectedness of an attack from behind, that gave Max the opportunity he had been looking for.

The man's guard was down, he half turned, with a ludicrous look of amazement and an unwary hand raised to his sore head. Max did not waste a moment. In seconds he had him wedged, face down over the car bonnet, both hands behind him, held in an iron grip.

'Who are you?' he snarled.

'John Butcher. Ouch!' Max had increased the pressure. 'Look, just let me go. I wasn't going to hurt anyone. This isn't worth the hassle.'

'Did my ex-husband put you up to this?' Kate demanded.

'What do you think?' the man spat out. 'Of course he did. I make a living snatching kids back for their parents. I

179

don't need this kind of bother, though.'

'You're despicable.' Max growled. 'A damned mercenary who doesn't mind hitting women.' He took a look at the blood still dripping from the cut on Kate's forehead and raised his arm angrily.

'No!' She grasped it before he brought it down. 'Two rights don't make a wrong. He isn't worth it. Let him go.'

The red mist of fury behind Max's eyes faded and his face relaxed. 'No, you're right.'

'What now?' Kate said and John Butcher, released from the hold Max had had on him, stood up, ruefully feeling the bump on his head and straightening his clothes.

'What now — is that I get out of here,' he said and walked to the saloon.

As Kate hurried to let Josef out, the whole car went by in a rush of squeaking tyres, the man inside making an obscene gesture as he passed them.

Kate drew the child to her in a

convulsive hug and turned to Max who had come quickly up to them.

Arms tightly around them both, he said, 'Thank God I didn't leave before.'

She looked up at him, gratitude shining in her eyes.

'If ever anyone ever paid a debt in full, Max, you did then. I'll never be able to thank you enough.'

He shook his head in denial but there was trouble in his face.

'Now all we have to do,' he said slowly, 'is wait for the next contingent!'

10

Kate was at the desk in the living-room the next day, trying to balance her budget, when she looked out of the window and saw a uniformed chauffeur opening the gate of the farm. He disappeared for a moment, then appeared again at the wheel of a sleek, black limousine. The vehicle edged its majestic way up the drive to park near the front door.

She was about to rush to the back of the house to warn Max when she saw who was being helped out of the car. Sirius's father — her ex father-in-law, Hassan! Kate could hardly believe it.

Gathering anger grew in her. How dare they! First they had tried to kidnap Josef and now, no doubt, the head of the family had come in person to persuade her to give up the child.

Well, he would find his mistake. He

had no rights in Britain. She had been given legal custody of her son and that was that. Except that she knew a craven relief because he had brought no entourage of strong arm followers with him. At least he didn't mean to use force.

When Hassan's chauffeur rang the bell and stood respectfully back to make room for his master, it was a dignified and composed Kate who opened the door to them.

Hassan was dressed with formality. For a moment each of them, he and Kate, gazed at each other with mutual dislike.

His English had always been perfect and now he announced, as one whose word was law, 'I have something to say to you — in private.'

Wishing she could refuse, but seeing no option other than to let him in, Kate stood back.

'Wait for me in the car,' he ordered the chauffeur and followed her into the living-room.

Once there he sat in a high-back chair and laid his gloves, meticulously tidily, on the table beside him.

'Sit down.' He said it as imperiously as though they were on his home ground instead of hers.

Kate obeyed, but burst out, 'How could you be so low as to pull that beastly trick yesterday? Trying to take Josef away from me.'

Hassan, in measured tones, said grimly, 'It does not matter to me whether you believe me or not, but I had nothing to do with that. I was displeased with my son when I discovered what he had done — had been doing for sometime.'

'Do you expect me to believe that?' Kate said contemptuously.

He stiffened. Opposition from a woman was something he neither expected nor approved of.

'As I have already told you, what you believe is of no interest to me. I have come for a purpose. It will be as well for you if you hear me out.'

Kate was silent.

He waited a moment and then continued, 'Josef is no longer to be a part of my — our — family.'

'What?' Kate was outraged. 'How dare you say that. He is Sirius' son, born during our marriage. Nothing can change that. You never wanted to acknowledge him because he was my child, too — and half-English — '

She could hardly get the words out, she was so incensed, but Hassan's expression remained totally impassive. Her justifiable resentment touched him not at all. He interrupted her unceremoniously.

'I did not say that I doubted he was my son's child. That is not the point. The reason I am here today is to insist that you, on his behalf, as his guardian so my lawyers tell me, through the British court — ' His lip curled. Clearly his opinion of a legal system which had been mad enough to appoint a woman custodian of a boy child, was extremely low. ' — should renounce any possibility

185

of his succeeding to my family rights and estates.'

That Josef was any kind of heir had not occurred to Kate. Getting away from them, and the abuse, had been all that mattered. Now, for the first time, she thought about it. They had lived, until now, on the small inheritance she had received from her parents. Would she, by agreeing to whatever he was suggesting, be taking away Josef's birthright?

'Why should I do that — if Josef is entitled to inherit something?'

Hassan's eyes flashed angrily.

'As I said, it would be as well for you to do so.'

Kate's blood ran cold. There could be no mistaking the threat in his words.

Seeing her sudden pallor, he looked smugly satisfied and drew a document from the inside pocket of his suit jacket.

'I have no intention of being ungenerous,' he assured her, suavely certain that she would accept his terms.

'As you see, my son and I, have

already placed our signatures here. I have been in Britain for five days. As soon as I return to my own country he will be coming with me — and marrying again — an eminently suitable bride this time. Their offspring will be — '

'Your first grandchildren.' Kate said with awful sarcasm. She was torn between intense bitterness on Josef's behalf, and a dawning sense of hope that perhaps at last they could be free.

Hassan, feeling no sense of shame whatsoever, bowed his head in agreement. 'My first grandchildren.' He said it proudly, looking her straight in the eye.

Kate took the paper he was holding out. She saw the sum that would be settled on Josef — and herself, for the duration of his childhood — and blinked. It would keep them in comparative luxury! If this was the pay-off, how much, she wondered dazedly, would she be voluntarily giving up if she accepted this offer? And would Josef, one day, reproach her for having done so?

What choice did she really have? The alternative was being hounded for years — or fighting costly battles through lawyers.

The document had clearly been drafted by a solicitor and everything seemed in order. There were two pages of it — she could do no more than skim her eyes over it, but the gist was clear. It was a promise that never again, once this was signed and the projected sum handed over, would she or her son be able to claim anything, have any rights or even be acknowledged as relatives of Hassan's family.

Having read it, she raised her eyes to the hard ones opposite her. Silently he handed her a fountain pen.

'Wait!'

Kate needed reassurance that she would indeed be free of the menace of her ex-husband.

'What about Sirius? You know — you always knew — how he treated me. How can I be sure that he still wouldn't come after us?'

Hassan looked steely.

'You need have no fear. Sirius will not disobey me. He looks forward to his new life, with anticipation. For him, as for all of us, the past is dead. You — and your son — do not exist.'

Kate did not know whether to burn with hatred for the extent of the bigotry which that statement exposed or to pity the girl who had been chosen by Hassan to be his new daughter-in-law.

She schooled her feelings of hostility and took the pen. What did it matter what they thought, or what their perception of the situation was? She knew the truth — and one day, when he was able to cope with it, Josef should be told the whole story. The important thing now, though, was to ensure that she and her son would be able to lead a normal life.

Without further hesitation she signed her name.

Hassan's limousine had only just slid

out of sight when Max hurried into the living-room, closely followed by Josef and Sam.

Kate was sitting by the desk in the window, holding her copy of the agreement and a cheque, the size of which she was still finding it hard to comprehend.

'Kate, I think I saw the tail end of a car? Has someone been here?'

He saw her face and came to her. 'Darling, what is it? You look as though you've seen a ghost?'

'No not a ghost — at least if it was, it was a very solid one.' She reached for Josef and drew him onto her lap, hugging him to her.

'Do you see this piece of paper, Josef? It will buy you a lot of things you've never been able to have before.'

'Sweets?' He asked hopefully, still regretful about the little bag of goodies which had landed on the grubby car floor yesterday and been inedible.

'Oh, yes!' Kate sighed dreamily. 'But a lot more than that.'

Max sat down in the chair vacated by Hassan.

'Something's happened. Tell me about it.'

For answer, Kate pushed the paper and the cheque towards him. Max scanned it. She watched his face, enjoying the range of expressions that crossed it, as he took in what this meant to her.

Josef had long since gone off to play with Benjy in the kitchen by the time Max finally looked up.

He didn't say anything at first, simply stood and gathered her to him. Thankfully, Kate put her arms about his waist.

He spoke to her quietly, 'So I take it this means that you're free from that villain at last?'

'Yes.' She sighed happily, her cheek nuzzling his sweater. 'Isn't it wonderful?'

'Wonderful,' he agreed but there was something in his voice that made her look up. He was gazing out of the window, his look serious and distant-focused.

Kate stood back, away from him. 'Max, aren't you happy for us?'

He tried to pull her back into his arms.

'Of course I am, my love, how could I not be?'

'You don't look it.'

A frisson of chill had crept down Kate's spine. Did he mind that only one of them was now a fugitive? She reproached herself for feeling so euphoric when his problems were still as great as ever. But it would have been strange had she not felt as though a weight had been lifted off her head.

Max, with an effort, smiled and held her by the shoulders, gently shaking her.

'You deserved this. The world will be your oyster from now on.'

'Yes, but I've already found a pearl,' Kate said.

He threw back his head and laughed. 'Are you talking about me? Thanks for the compliment, but the main thing is for me to get going. You're safe now, sweet Kate, and I can leave you with a clear conscience.'

'And an empty heart,' Kate said bleakly, but he wouldn't allow her to fall into depression, setting himself, for the rest of the day, the task of keeping her cheerful with plans for how she would set up a life — with or without me, he told her steadily, depending on what happens when I get to London.

'What are you going to do there?' She asked curiously, when they were alone, at ten o'clock that evening.

'See my lawyer.' Max was certain about that. 'He was a friend and always believed in me — in spite of the evidence. He won't give me away until I've had the chance to see Dinah.'

Taking her chin in his hand and gazing deep into her eyes he said, 'Do you realise that you've never once asked me for details of why I was imprisoned. Any other woman would have wanted every last gruesome detail.'

'Once I knew you, I trusted you,' Kate said simply. 'Then I loved you — but who is Dinah?'

'My ex-partner's wife.' Max's face had clouded, as he broodingly recalled the circumstances which had led to his arrest.

'Clare, my wife, went off with Jason, my partner. They also took the contents of our joint bank account, and the whole of the business account and profits. We'd just sold the antique shop we shared — Jason and I, so that was a considerable sum. I was a fool to trust either of them. I swore I'd never trust anyone again. Then, after two months of silence, she rang me. Told me where she was — a flat in Kensington — said she was frightened — and asked me to come.'

'You went?'

Kate was almost afraid to stop the flow of information. She had been curious but had forbore to ask questions because of his sensitivity. She had wanted to do or ask nothing which sounded as though she doubted his innocence.

'Yes I went.'

Max was silent for a moment as visions of the scene he had found swept over him. His face darkened.

'She was already dead — strangled. The door was open. I hadn't been there more than a few minutes — stupidly trying to revive her — when the police arrived. I had the means, the motive — and the opportunity. They really had no choice other than to arrest me.'

'Oh, Max. It must have been absolutely dreadful. But who do you think had really done it?'

'Jason. I'm pretty sure of it.' Max's mouth was set in a thin line.

'He was given an alibi by his wife. Only lately she's had a change of heart. She wrote to me in jail, not really saying anything, but clearly feeling remorseful. I believe that if I could get to her now — persuade her — she's ripe for finally telling the truth. She wasn't a bad sort, poor Dinah. It's my belief that Jason is up to his old womanising tricks again and she's had enough. A statement from her would let Barney — my friend and lawyer — re-open the case, with new evidence.'

Kate was secretly horrified at the flimsiness of his hopes. Everything — both of their futures — were dependant upon the word of a woman who had already admitted to perjuring herself! Still, if it was his only chance then she must support him fully.

'Take the Carney's car when you go,' she said quietly. 'Now that I have money to buy them a new one if necessary, it's the best thing to do. And the cash I have left is yours, too. I'll be opening a bank account tomorrow.'

'I hate to do that, but I can't afford to refuse. Once I've seen Barney I can arrange for funds through him. Until then — '

He took her face in his hands and scrutinised every detail as though he were committing every facet of her to memory.

'Whatever happens, darling, remember that I love you.'

It was only the next day, when he had gone, and Kate spent the lonely time, replaying the scenario of their last few hours together, that she realised the terrifying finality of those words and knew, with horrifying clarity, that Max might not return!

Without Max, the days were appallingly empty! Josef, who had got used to a father figure, missed him as much as she did and was fretful and mopey. With no more need to hide away, Kate tried to involve herself with village affairs, accepting invitations when she could, and gratefully joining now friends for coffee or afternoon tea. Even now, though, she had to be wary. As one secret had gone, another had taken its place.

Two weeks passed and she had bought a car, enrolled Josef in the playgroup and been to Tavistock to indulge herself in a shopping spree. Buying new clothes was a pleasure, but it seemed a pointless exercise when Max wasn't there to see her in them. She longed — oh, how she longed — to bring things home to show him and see his eyes light up in appreciation.

Soon there were signs of Spring on the branches of the trees, as early catkins appeared and blue crocus peeped demurely out in the Carney's garden.

Life could have been so good, but the ice in Kate's heart could not be melted. She went about like an automaton, smiling, playing with Josef, looking after the animals, the house and the garden, trying to ignore the hollow desolation inside her.

He rang just once.

'Max!' She was overjoyed to hear his voice. 'What's happening?'

He was guarded. 'It — it isn't going too well, darling. Barney has been great. He's working fantastically hard — but Dinah — I don't know if — ' He broke off, then said emphatically, 'Kate, if I can't — I want you to get on with your life and forget me.'

'Don't say things like that.' She was appalled. 'If seeing you means prison visits, then that's what I'll do.'

'No, never.' It was a firm denial, then a silence.

'Max, speak to me.' She was pleading. She heard him sigh.

'Good-night, sweet Kate. Goodbye, my darling.'

The phone clicked, and she knew he had rung off.

She was in despair, knowing she could not contact him, sensing the chivalrous instinct that made him determined to stay out of her life unless he succeeded in his quest to prove his innocence. Almost, she hated him for not recognising that what she really wanted was to see him — anywhere, anyhow!

★   ★   ★

There was another two weeks of living life on automatic pilot before the sun finally shone.

She had driven Josef down to the village and left him at his playgroup for two hours. Back at the farm she was weeding the borders in front of the living-room windows. The Carney's would be back before long and she wanted them to find everything in apple-pie order. She hoped they would not be upset by being presented with a new car instead of their old one!

As she knelt on the path, busy with the trowel, a shadow fell across the earth in front of her. A well-remembered, well-loved voice said teasingly, 'There's no need to kneel at my feet, you know.'

Kate whirled around. The sun was in her eyes, she shaded them with one hand.

'Max — oh, Max, you've come back.'

He jerked her to her feet and held her to him, burying his face in her hair and saying thickly. 'I've longed for this moment since the day I went away.'

Kate held back a little, the better to look at him.

'You look so handsome,' she said shakily. 'I'd hardly have recognised you.'

'That's what wearing my own clothes, instead of Jim's, does for me,' Max told her. He was looking deep into her eyes as though he wanted to search for the core of her being, but he only said lightly, 'You look different, too. I knew you'd make a lovely blonde — though a slightly earthy one at this moment.'

Lovingly, he rubbed a patch of soil from her cheek.

'Is it all right then?' She hardly dared ask.

He nodded. 'I wouldn't be here if it weren't. There are lots of formalities to go through, but I'm a free man.'

'Free!' Kate breathed. Such a vast relief washed through her that tears of joy threatened to overcome her.

Max said, 'We're so lucky to have found each other. Isn't it strange, sweet Kate, that we were both running away — both trying to fight for the right to live our lives.'

'We're not running anymore,' Kate whispered.

Max's desire to kiss her could be contained no longer. He brought his mouth close to her waiting one, but before their lips met, he murmured, 'No, Kate. Now it's time to stop running.'

THE END